Praise for Maya Banks's *Colters' Daughter*

"I can't begin to express the complete contentment I feel after reading *Colters' Daughter*... A beautiful story for striking characters. I dare you to read it just once!"

~ *Joyfully Reviewed*

"If money were no object, I would buy all three books in the series for all my friends because they are worth reading. Even though this book is a stand-alone story, after completing it I wanted to pull out the first two and read them all over again."

~ *Whipped Cream Reviews*

"Keep ice on hand as you read *Colters' Daughter* as Max and Callie burn up the pages."

~ *Literary Nymphs*

"Ms. Banks has always done an amazing job of bringing the characters and their stories to life, and this book is no different... This is one book and one series you definitely will want to read."

~ *The Romance Studio*

Look for these titles by
Maya Banks

Now Available:

Seducing Simon
Love Me, Still
Long Road Home

Brazen
Reckless *(stand-alone sequel to Brazen)*

Unbroken
Understood
Overheard
Undenied

Falcon Mercenary Group
Into the Mist
Into the Lair

Linger
Stay With Me
Songbird

Wild
Golden Eyes
Amber Eyes

Print Anthologies
The Perfect Gift
Caught by Cupid
Red-Hot Summer

Print Collections
Unbroken
Linger
Wild

Colters' Legacy
Colters' Woman
Colters' Lady
Colters' Daughter

Free Download:

AT
SamhainPublishing.com
Colters' Wife

Colters' Daughter

Maya Banks

Samhain Publishing, Ltd.
11821 Mason Montgomery Road, 4B
Cincinnati, OH 45249
www.samhainpublishing.com

Colters' Daughter

Print ISBN: 978-1-60928-394-0
Digital ISBN: 978-1-60928-025-3

Editing by Jennifer Miller
Cover by Natalie Winters

First Samhain Publishing, Ltd. electronic publication: February 2011
First Samhain Publishing, Ltd. print publication: February 2012

Dedication

For Jilly, Inez and Amy, three very sweet ladies who've been very good to me.

Chapter One

The Mountain Pass Bar and Grill was hopping like frogs during mating season. It was early summer and past ski season, but the little town of Clyde still managed to pull tourists from the larger neighboring towns. Not to mention, Friday was local's night when all the residents of Clyde decided to let their hair down and imbibe a little.

Callie Colter slid another drink down the bar to a waiting customer then loaded up her waitress's tray with a round of draft beers and sent her back into the crowd.

Taking advantage of the momentary lull in the action, Callie leaned back against the counter and surveyed the mass of people packed into The Mountain Pass. The live band pounded out a raucous country song that had the dance floor filled to capacity with people line dancing. A skill Callie had never felt it necessary to learn. Nor had she the ability. She had the rhythm of a slug.

And really, the whole line-dancing thing? She was still scarred from having to watch a really hokey George Strait movie—courtesy of her brothers.

Her mother swore Callie was the cosmopolitan one in the family. Callie had been all over the world, but the reality was she was a homebody at heart and there was no better place than the sanctuary of her family—as oddball as it was.

And so here she was, licking her wounds and brooding about asshole males. Quite amusing when you considered she had three—yes *three*—fathers and three brothers, and none of them fell under the asshole label, and no, she wasn't being biased. It didn't mean the rest of the male population didn't suffer the disease though.

She reached down to wipe her hands on the towel hanging from her waist when the music stopped. She glanced up to see the drummer motion to her that they were taking five. She nodded and set about getting the band members a round of beer.

"Hello, Callie."

The husky voice whispered over her ears and sent chill bumps down her neck. She froze, her hand still on the tap.

It couldn't be. No way Max was here in her little town, in Dillon's bar.

She yanked her hand back and swore when beer foamed over the glass. Then she whipped her head up, sure she'd imagined that voice.

A pair of hunter green eyes fringed by a set of dark lashes that would make a female weep in envy stared penetratingly back at her. She stared, mouth open, at Max Wilder who stood arrogantly across the bar like he expected her to fall at his feet or squeal in delight to see him.

It would be a cold day in hell before she'd do either.

She narrowed her eyes, and he must have gotten some hint of the welcome he was about to receive because he held a hand up as if to ward her off.

"We need to talk, Callie."

"Bullshit."

His eyes widened in surprise. She leaned forward and

crooked her finger for him to come closer. Eyeing her warily, he bent toward her and looked like he was about to speak again.

She balled her fist and swung as hard as she could. His head snapped back, and pain exploded in her fingers.

He grabbed at his jaw and staggered back. "Son of a bitch! Goddamn, Callie, give me a chance to explain."

"You've got two seconds to get the hell out of my bar or I'm calling the cops. And did I mention that my brother's the sheriff?"

Carl, her bouncer, thrust his huge body between Max and the bar, blocking Callie's view. "You heard the lady. Beat it."

Callie craned to see around Carl. Still rubbing his jaw, Max took a step back, his eyes glittering as he stared at Callie.

He glanced sideways at the mountain that was Carl then back to Callie and lifted one brow. "Do you honestly think that he'll keep me from you?"

Callie frowned. Carl bristled and took a step in Max's direction. Max didn't look overly worried—a fact that worried Callie plenty.

Max was a badass. It wasn't that he looked like one. He wasn't overly muscled and didn't have a tree trunk for a neck like Carl did. But he was fast and unafraid. He knew he was a badass, which made him even more of one in Callie's eyes.

His jaw was set in a tight line that made him look stubborn. She'd seen that look often enough. She'd also tasted that strong jaw. She'd licked a path from his mouth to his ear and nibbled at all parts in between. She could still feel the faint rasp of his beard on her tongue, for God's sake.

She'd also witnessed what happened when Max got pissed off.

"Don't make me call my brother, Max. You can't think it's

worth spending the night in jail."

His nostrils flared for a moment as his gaze bore into her. He ought to know that she didn't make empty threats. She could be just as stubborn as he was. Lord knew they'd butted heads often enough, and she'd never backed down. Except in the bedroom. Always in the bedroom.

Heat flushed through her body, and she hoped to hell the neon lighting around the bar disguised her blush. The last thing she wanted to do was show any sign that he'd flustered her with his sudden appearance.

"This isn't finished," he bit out.

"The hell it's not. I have nothing to say to you, Max."

For a minute she actually thought there was genuine pain in his eyes that had nothing to do with the fact she'd hit him in the face. Which was absurd given that he'd fucked her over, not the other way around.

She flexed her fingers and rubbed at her hand as Carl escorted Max out the front door.

"I'm beginning to think you have anger management issues, Callie," Paul Woodrow drawled as he leaned against the bar next to her.

Callie scowled at the part-time bartender. Nice of him to show up now. If he'd been to work on time, she wouldn't have been here when Max came in.

"I didn't throw him through the window."

Paul chuckled. "Good thing. Dillon wouldn't be happy if he had to replace more glass."

She shook her aching hand and turned to the side to collect herself. She was more shaken by Max's appearance than she'd like to admit. Seeing him again after so long had been a complete shock. Why would he turn up now? He didn't even grovel. He'd practically ordered her to talk to him. As if.

Max didn't yell orders. He never raised his voice. He didn't have to. She'd been more than happy to do anything he wanted. She cringed and squeezed her eyes shut. Yeah, she'd been more than happy to accommodate him, and all it had gotten her was a healthy dose of stupid.

She opened her eyes to see Paul eyeing her curiously as he made drinks. She frowned and turned away. A few months before, right after she'd slunk home to crawl under a rock, she'd thrown a smart-ass college kid through the front window of the bar.

The upside was that people were reluctant to start shit when she was tending bar. The downside was that now her family watched her even closer for signs she was going to start barking at the moon or frothing at the mouth.

"You okay, Callie?" Carl asked sharply.

She glanced up. "Yeah. No big deal. I took care of it."

"Want me to call Dillon?"

She shook her head and frowned. "I took care of it. No reason to bug Dillon. I'm perfectly capable of running the bar. The last thing I need is him or Seth hovering over me when I'm trying to work."

Carl grunted. "Having the sheriff around isn't a bad thing."

"Oh come on." She snorted. "Nothing happens around here. Ever since Seth took over as sheriff, it's been boring as hell. Tonight was as much excitement as Clyde's seen since I threw the dude through the window. Everyone will thank me for breaking up the monotony."

"So who was he?"

Callie's lips tightened. "No one important."

For several long minutes, she stared at the door where Max

had departed. Why had he come? Why now? She'd wasted far too much time moping over him. Chalk it up to age and lack of experience on her part, but it wasn't a mistake she planned to make again.

Max Wilder could drag himself back off to Italy or Greece or wherever the hell it was he ditched her. She was embarrassed to remember just how long she waited for him to come back before she got a clue and realized he'd dumped her.

"You heading out now, Callie? I can take it from here," Paul said.

"Yeah, I know you can," she muttered. "It's busy, though. I'll hang around in case there are any more problems."

She didn't particularly want to be *here*, but she didn't want to walk out that door and chance Max being *there*, waiting for her. It was one thing to take him on inside a crowded bar. Face to face? Not that he would hurt her. But he wasn't a man who took no for an answer when he wanted something. Callie wasn't sure what he wanted, exactly, and she'd be an idiot to find out.

By the time she closed up at two a.m., she was exhausted and didn't have it in her to drive up the mountain to her parents' cabin. Nor did she want to go crash on her brothers' couch. They'd all be asleep.

Callie chuckled. It amazed her that her mother had managed to hook up with three men. Lily, her sister-in-law, had done the same with Callie's brothers, and here Callie couldn't even manage a relationship with one man.

She was sure the townspeople, and hell, maybe even her own family, wondered if she harbored the desire to marry more than one man. There was probably a betting pool somewhere on how many men she would end up with.

She loved her fathers and her brothers dearly, but she had no idea how her mom and Lily managed it. Having more than one man in the house would drive her out of her mind. Too much testosterone. Too many moody males to contend with. Too many egos. Too much posturing, bickering and all-around aggravation.

Her mom and Lily were happy though, so Callie was all for it. For them. As long as she wasn't expected to keep with the bizarre tradition.

She trudged back to Dillon's office after turning off the lights. He had a couch that he sometimes slept on—well, that was before Lily came into the picture. Nowadays he rushed home every afternoon to spend time with his new wife. One or two nights a week, he came in to work the bar to give Callie a night off, but the truth was, nights off just gave her more time to think stupid shit. If she stayed busy, she didn't think up acceptable reasons why Max dumped her cold in a foreign country.

She fished a bottle of water out of the minifridge by Dillon's desk and then settled on the couch. She didn't even bother to undress. She propped her feet up on the end, drained the bottle of water and then leaned back to close her eyes.

And all she could see was that moment where she looked up and saw Max standing just across the bar from her looking as sexy as ever.

She'd been utterly fascinated by him from the day she met him. He was older, a bit stern, but he had just enough rough edges to his polished look to make her drool. He was strong and confident, and oh but confidence on a man was super sexy.

He liked things his way, and really, so did she. Now, looking back, she was mortified by just how much control she gave up around him. No one who knew her would ever believe the woman she'd become in his arms.

That's what bothered her the most. He'd made her someone

else, he'd made her need him, and then he'd walked away.

And now he thought they had something to talk about?

She growled under her breath. "Go to sleep, Callie. You'll go see Lily tomorrow and you'll feel better."

Unfortunately, she obeyed herself about as well as she obeyed everyone else.

Max Wilder examined his jaw in the mirror and shook his head. A chuckle escaped and then he winced. The little wench had caught his bottom lip in the punch.

He shouldn't have expected any less from Callie. She was fiery, impulsive, she grabbed onto life with both hands, she loved fiercely, but she was also capable of holding a grudge forever.

With a sigh he trudged out of the bathroom with a towel around his hips. Accommodations were mediocre at best in Clyde. Hell, he was lucky to have gotten a room at all given the fact that there was only one hotel.

There were much nicer towns that had more appeal for tourists but then he wouldn't be close to Callie. He had a lot of ground to cover with her, and judging by tonight, it was going to take some fast talking. The woman was lethal.

And she was so damn beautiful, she made his chest ache.

He'd missed her. Every damn day they'd been apart, he missed her until she was all that consumed his thoughts. Forgotten was the reason why he'd initially pursued her. That no longer mattered. It hadn't mattered since the first time he'd made love to her and recognized his other half.

It was corny. Overwrought. And he didn't give a damn. Callie was his. He'd made mistakes. Mistakes that had cost them both more than he could ever imagine. But she was his, and he had every intention of reasserting his claim on her.

It bordered on obsession. His need to possess her. To mark her. To stake his claim—again. This time... This time he wouldn't let her go. Not ever again.

He simply wasn't whole without her.

Pain—and regret—weighed heavy on his heart. The idea that he'd forego a promise made to the man who'd raised him as his own, that he'd lay aside the request of his dying mother. Her whispered apology that she hadn't held on to the legacy that should belong to him and his sister and to their children.

He considered himself an honorable man. A man who put his family above all else. But what he'd done—what he'd considered doing—to Callie wasn't honorable. Never mind that he hadn't—couldn't—go through with it.

Breaking his word was also not honorable, but from the moment he'd laid eyes on Callie, held her in his arms, taken what she'd so sweetly offered, he'd known. He'd known that he couldn't have her *and* his honor when it came to his family.

He'd chosen Callie.

He'd always choose Callie.

He just had to convince her of that fact without her ever knowing the true reason for their chance meeting in Europe. It would only hurt her, and Max would do anything in the world to never hurt her again as he'd done by leaving. Even though his reasons were solid and he'd had much to consider in the time they were apart.

She thought he hadn't loved her enough.

The truth was he loved her too damn much.

Chapter Two

Callie woke with a sore back and a grumpy disposition. She hated sleeping on the couch. Which was kind of funny when she thought of some of the places she'd slept when she traveled. She'd slept in train stations, hostels with creaky cots, and she'd done plenty of camping. But a couch? She'd rather sleep on the ground.

She stumbled out of Dillon's office, checked her watch and decided it wasn't too early to head to Lily's.

What she really needed was a place of her own. Not that she minded staying with her folks. She loved them to pieces and her fathers doted on her shamelessly. She split her time between her parents' and Lily and her brothers' house, but they really couldn't accommodate her long-term. Not until the renovations were completed. And by then she hoped to be closer to her own dream.

She'd promised herself, though, that she'd save every penny she earned to build her dream house in Callie's Meadow, the piece of land she was born on. Land that had been gifted to her by her parents.

She traveled a lot. She'd always been a restless spirit, but she traveled very economically, and she always knew that one day she'd settle here on the mountain, surrounded by her family.

In the meantime, she built her savings and dreamed of the house she'd build in her meadow.

It was a toss-up as to whether she wanted to drive up to her parents' to grab a shower and make herself more presentable before going over to Dillon's to see Lily or just show up at her brothers' and risk them giving her the third degree.

At least there she had Lily to side with her, and dealing with her overprotective big brothers was a lot better than a worried mama. Holly Colter was like a lioness when it came to her children. No matter how grown up they were, they were still her cubs and she treated them accordingly.

Callie smiled as she thought of her mom. Sometimes there was nothing sweeter than a mother's hug. It really did make everything better.

She'd go up later to visit her mom and say hello to her dads. But for now she'd head over to see Lily, grab a shower there and do some venting.

Lily was one of the sweetest people Callie knew. She just had this way of looking at you that made you feel like everything would be okay. And she'd been through hell on earth. Callie respected that. She'd know exactly where Callie was coming from and she'd listen. Right now Callie really needed someone to listen.

She hopped into her mini-SUV, the same one she'd driven since getting her driver's license, and pulled away from the bar. The dads made noises about getting her a new truck. They didn't like the fact that she drove such an old vehicle. But it ran great and the body was in excellent condition. There was no need for a new one. She couldn't afford one, and she didn't want her parents footing the bill even though they could well afford it.

She'd paid her own way since striking out on her own. That

wasn't going to change.

She knew her parents were disappointed that she hadn't followed in her brothers' footsteps and gone to college, but she'd always known university wasn't for her. She was simply too rebellious and too restless to ever survive four years in school. High school had been bad enough.

She was smart, and she wasn't afraid of hard work. All she really needed was her house on her land. As soon as she had the money for that, she could continue traveling and picking up jobs here and there, and she'd always have her refuge to come back to.

If Dillon couldn't give her enough work, she could always help Michael out in his veterinary practice. It was growing in leaps and bounds, and he'd be even busier when the only other vet in town retired next year.

It seemed everyone in her family was settled but Callie.

Seth was finally home where he belonged after working as a Denver police officer. After he'd met Lily, he'd moved back to Clyde and taken the position of sheriff from Lacey England who'd retired because of her husband's ill health.

Callie had been on her way to healing. She'd licked her wounds for far too long as it was. She had finally achieved a modicum of peace. And now Max had shown up and taken it all away.

Damn the man.

She pulled into the drive of Dillon's cabin and parked between the multitudes of trucks. She didn't even try to straighten her appearance. She knew she looked like she was hungover but there was little she could do about it at this point.

She trudged up the steps and knocked. A few moments later, Dillon opened the door and stared at her with that big-brother look that always made her squirm.

"Rough night at the bar?"

She pushed by him. "Yeah, something like that. Is Lily here?"

"She's painting," Dillon said. "But you can go in. She's always glad to see you."

Callie smiled at that. The feeling was entirely mutual. Lily was just...special. She started to walk away but Dillon called after her.

"Are you going to tell me what went on at the bar?"

"I didn't throw anyone through the window. I didn't break anything and I didn't have to call Seth. So there's nothing you need to worry about."

"So says you."

She ignored him and went back to the office that Dillon had converted into an art room for Lily. She knocked and then stuck her head inside to see Lily staring at her canvas, her bottom lip caught between her teeth in determined concentration.

"Can I come in?"

Lily glanced up and a wide smile broke over her face. "Callie! Of course you can. It's wonderful to see you." Then she frowned. "What on earth happened to you?"

Callie smiled wryly. "Can I borrow your shower and maybe a change of clothes? I didn't feel like going all the way up to Mom's. I spent the night in Dillon's office and I look and feel like crap."

Concern crinkled Lily's forehead. "Of course you can. Take whatever you'd like out of my closet."

"Thanks. I'll be back in a few minutes."

Callie headed into the bedroom where Lily kept her clothes and found her brother Michael sprawled across the bed reading a book.

"Hey kiddo," Michael said as he looked over his book. "What are you doing?"

"Lily said I could borrow some clothes and use the shower."

He frowned and studied her for a minute. "Not that I ever mind you coming over here, but why on earth do you look like you slept in those clothes?"

"Because I did? I crashed in Dillon's office last night. Was late closing up. Didn't feel like driving home."

"You should have carried your ass over here," he growled. "There's no reason for you to have slept in the bar. What if someone broke in and tried to rob the place, for God's sake?"

She rolled her eyes and headed into the bathroom, shutting the door before he could really get wound up. She loved her brothers dearly, and she'd always been especially close to Seth, but there were just some things she couldn't talk to them about. Max being one of them because they'd want to go kick his ass, and if they knew he was here, there'd be no holding them back.

She didn't spend long in the shower, just long enough to wash her hair and remove the grimy feel from her skin. Alcohol and cigarette smoke did that to you.

After dressing in a pair of sweats—because Lily was too tiny for Callie to fit into her jeans—and one of Seth's T-shirts, she wrapped a towel around her head and went back into the bedroom, relieved that Michael was no longer there. Of course he'd probably gone to find Dillon and Seth so they could gang up on her later.

She slipped down the hall and into Lily's office and shut the door. Lily looked up. "Feel better?"

"Ten times," Callie said. "Thanks."

Callie walked over and sat down on the floor in front of

where Lily was painting and put her palms back to brace herself. "What are you working on?"

Lily frowned and made a sound of exasperation. "I wish I knew. It feels like a big blob of nothing. I'm not sure what the hell I was thinking."

"I'm sure it's beautiful."

Lily smiled. "You're so sweet to me and so good for my ego. Between you and the guys, I'll be convinced that I'm the next Picasso."

Callie leaned further back until she was flat on the floor. Then she put her hands behind her head and stared up at the ceiling. "Can I ask you something, Lily?"

She heard Lily put her paintbrush aside.

"Of course."

"When you went to see Charles...did it feel good to tell him off? Or did it make you feel worse?"

Callie glanced over to see Lily's startled look. Charles was Lily's ex-husband and a complete bastard. He'd placed the blame on Lily for the loss of their daughter, and Callie had never been more proud of Lily than when she went to confront him and tell him how wrong he'd been.

Lily's brows drew together and she pursed her lips in thought. "I don't really know, to be honest. It was such an emotional day for me. I remember feeling betrayed when I saw he had a new wife and new children. I was angry. But by the time it was over, I was just sad. I suppose I was more relieved than anything. Why do you ask?"

Callie closed her eyes. She wasn't sure how she felt after telling Max what she thought of him. The problem was, Lily wasn't in love with Charles—she hadn't been for years. Callie couldn't say the same about Max. Oh, she wanted to hate him.

She did in some ways. But his betrayal still cut deep. It was still fresh. In some ways, it was just yesterday.

"Callie?" Lily softly prompted.

Callie sighed. "Remember I told you I fell hard for someone and that he dumped me after taking what he wanted?"

Lily scowled. "Yes, I remember."

"I met him when I was in Europe. His name was Max. He was... He was perfect. Or so I thought. He was handsome. Confident. Arrogant. He was strong and so dominant he made me shiver just being in the same room with him."

Lily quietly got up and sat on the floor beside Callie. She lay down so they were side by side and reached over to take Callie's hand.

"I fell so fast. He seemed so into me, so in tune with my needs. I gave him complete control in the bedroom," she said quietly. "I felt so cherished. He took such good care of me. He told me he wanted us to be together. I thought he was the one. I mean, I almost called Mom to tell her I had met the man I was going to marry. I know that sounds horribly naive now. I cringe when I think of how stupid and foolish I was."

Lily squeezed her hand. "Don't. Don't be ashamed because you gave him your heart."

Callie squeezed back, her chest tightening at the comfort Lily gave without even realizing it. "We spent three wonderful weeks together. It was all such a blur. Italy, Greece, we explored so much. We spent every moment together and every night in his bed. It was like a fairy tale. I've never been happier.

"Then one day he said he'd gotten a phone call and he had to go back to the U.S. for an emergency. He didn't give me details. He was in such a hurry to leave, but before he did, he told me to wait. That he'd be back in a few days, a week at the most. He'd come back and then we'd be together. He wanted me to enjoy the rest of my vacation.

"He never came back."

Lily gripped Callie's hand tighter. "I hate him."

Callie laughed even as the sting of tears made her nose draw up. "You don't hate anyone, Lily. Not even Charles, and if there was ever a reason to hate someone, he would be it."

Lily sniffed. "I do so hate Max. He's a bastard for hurting you. I think we should tell the guys so they can go beat him up. Seth could find him for you."

"He's here," Callie whispered.

Lily sat up and looked down at Callie, her eyes wide. "Here? Where?"

"He came into the bar last night."

Lily scowled ferociously and she looked so cute, Callie giggled despite the tension in the air.

"So he left you in Europe, never came back—did he call you?"

Callie shook her head. "I waited. I waited for an entire month. I canceled the rest of my trip to the other parts of Europe I was backpacking through because I wanted to be there where he asked me to wait. I spent every dime I had on the hotel because I was worried he'd come back and I wouldn't be there. He never called. When I finally made myself face the fact that he wasn't coming back and that he'd played me, I was devastated. I couldn't even be that angry at him because I'd made it so disgustingly easy for him. I was furious with myself."

"Oh no, Callie." Tears shone in Lily's eyes as she crossed her legs and gathered Callie's hand in hers. "You can't blame yourself because he was an asshole. What the hell did he want last night? He's got a lot of nerve showing up here after what he did."

Lily was vibrating with indignation and Callie wanted to sit up and squeeze the life out of her. It felt so good to have someone to confide in, someone to offer her unconditional support.

"I don't know what he wants," Callie admitted. "He said he wanted to talk. He didn't ask. He just demanded. He's used to getting what he wants. I decked him and told him to get lost."

Lily's hand flew to her mouth and her eyes shone with merriment. "You hit him? Really?"

Callie nodded.

Lily burst into laughter. "Oh my God, I wish I could have been there to see it!"

Then her laughter died and fury entered her gaze. "He didn't hurt you, did he? Did he touch you in any way? I swear if he did, I'm going to have Seth arrest him. After Michael and Dillon beat the crap out of him."

Callie chuckled. "You're so bloodthirsty, Lily. I like it. No, he didn't hurt me. Whatever he may have done to me emotionally, he'd never hurt me physically. He... He was always extremely careful not to hurt me. When we were together he was so...protective. He was so focused on me."

Lily pulled at Callie's arm until Callie sat up. Then Lily hugged her fiercely and Callie clung to her. "I'm so sorry, Callie. He doesn't deserve you."

Callie slowly pulled away. "No, he doesn't deserve me. I deserve better than what he did. But it still hurts and I don't know how to make that go away. I can't handle seeing him. I thought I had pulled myself together. But then I saw him again and it all came back."

Lily pulled her back into a hug and rocked back and forth. "I don't know how to make it stop hurting. It's not something you can just turn off. It takes time."

"Lily? Callie? Is something wrong?"

Callie jerked her gaze to the door to see Seth standing there, a frown etched deep into his face. Lily squeezed her reassuringly and then turned to her husband.

"It's girl stuff."

Seth didn't look impressed or put off by Lily's explanation.

"What kind of girl stuff?"

"I just needed to talk to Lily," Callie said. "I knew she'd make me feel better and she has."

Seth wasn't pleased by being blown off. He glared at both of them. Lily picked herself up off the floor and then reached down to help Callie.

"I'm willing to bet that Dillon has breakfast cooked which is why Seth came in here to begin with. Am I right?" Lily asked as she turned to her husband.

He gave a short nod.

Lily took Callie's hand and then pulled her up to her side so she could wrap her arm around Callie's waist.

"Then let's go get something to eat. I'm starving and I bet you are too, Callie. You never eat well when you work the bar."

Callie grinned at the fussy note she heard in Lily's voice. It warmed her to her toes.

"Have I ever told you how good you did picking this one, big brother?" Callie asked as she and Lily walked past him.

"Don't think I'm letting this drop," Seth said in a terse voice. "I want to know what the hell is going on with you, Callie."

Callie rolled her eyes and continued down the hall with Lily at her side.

Chapter Three

Lunch was uncomfortable despite Lily's warm presence and reassuring manner. Callie's three brothers stared holes through her until she felt taken apart piece by piece. It was all she could do to calmly eat her meal and pretend that her world hadn't shifted on its axis the night before.

Midway through, Dillon sighed and put down his fork. "I think you should take tonight off, Callie. If I can't find a bartender to cover for you, I'll go in myself."

"Okay."

She instantly regretted her easy acquiescence. The agreement had slipped out born of her relief that she wouldn't have to face a night when Max could very well show up again thinking to ambush her. Instead she should have made a show of arguing and then grudgingly relenting. Because now her brothers would be convinced that something was horribly wrong.

"I thought I'd go up to Mom's," she said in an attempt to cover the sudden silence. "She's been nagging me about being home for meals, but I've been working so much that I haven't had the chance."

Michael and Dillon might have been convinced by her explanation but Seth studied her with complete disbelief.

"I'd like to go in with you, Dillon," Lily spoke up.

Dillon arched a brow and Callie nearly groaned. Fiercely loyal Lily wanted to go because her protective instincts had been riled by Callie's account of her relationship with Max. Now Lily would be looking for Max, and hell, she'd probably make good on her threat to have Seth arrest him if she saw him in the bar.

"Not that I mind you going anywhere with me, sweetness, but what's the occasion? Saturdays at Mountain Pass can be loud and obnoxious. It's not really a place I like you being."

Lily frowned and Callie glanced over, her eyes pleading with Lily to forget she'd ever heard about Max Wilder. Lily stared back at Callie and then sighed.

"It was just a thought." She lifted her shoulder in a shrug. "Maybe some other time."

Dillon matched Lily's frown. "It's not that I don't want you with me. I hope you know that. I'd just rather you be here with Michael and Seth where I know you're safe."

Lily rolled her eyes. "For God's sake, Dillon. What do you think would happen if I went into a bar? I used to live on the streets, for God's sake."

All three men scowled at the reminder that the woman they loved had spent three heartbreaking years homeless after suffering a devastating loss. It made Callie's heart twist too, and just the image that Lily invoked made Callie reach over and squeeze her hand.

Lily looked at them all in bewilderment for a moment before she seemed to realize why they'd reacted. Her expression softened and then she smiled at each in turn. "If I hadn't lived on the streets, if I hadn't experienced the sorrow I did, I would have never found and loved all of you."

"That doesn't mean we want to even think of you being out there hungry and alone," Michael muttered.

Callie sympathized with her brothers. So much of Lily's past she seemed to take in stride. She'd blossomed from wounded bird to a fierce eagle. She seemed so complacent and at peace with her past, and yet it still bothered her husbands immensely. Not a day went by that they didn't do all they could to make Lily feel loved and cherished.

She sighed. Watching her fathers with her mother and her brothers with Lily brought home all the things she wanted in a man. All the things she thought she'd found in Max. Maybe she'd expected too much. Maybe they'd broken the mold when the Colter men were fashioned. Maybe no one would ever live up to the example set by her fathers and brothers.

It was a depressing thought because after witnessing just how much her mother and Lily were adored by their husbands, Callie knew she could never settle for anything less than what they'd found.

Her chest ached and she had the strangest urge to cry all over again. She'd sworn she was done grieving for Max, but she felt worse today knowing that he was just a few miles away than she had when she'd first come home to nurse the wounds he'd inflicted on her.

She pushed up from the table, no longer trusting herself to keep it together in front of her brothers. She made a point of taking her plate into the kitchen so that it would appear as if she'd simply finished her meal.

She scraped the half-eaten food into the trash and then turned the water on in the sink to rinse it. She was staring at the rushing water when Seth put a hand on her shoulder.

"What's bothering you, baby?"

Her heart ached at the endearment. Seth had called her baby since she was a toddler. She'd adored him growing up. Always the oldest. Always the one in charge. Michael and Dillon had tormented him relentlessly, but he'd always been the one Callie could run to when the chips were down.

He'd held her hand on her first day of kindergarten despite the fact he was at an age where being seen with his younger sister was decidedly uncool. He'd walked her all the way to class and had been there at the end of the day to walk her down the street to the sheriff's department where their mom picked them up.

There'd never been a time when she'd held back from him. He'd nursed her through countless crushes. He'd sympathized when she'd had her heart broken by her prom date and even offered to escort her to the dance himself. As if she'd really show up with her brother. Instead they'd downloaded movies and spent the evening eating junk food and laughing over ridiculous disaster movies.

But now she simply couldn't communicate the depth of her heartache to him. It wasn't that she didn't trust him. It had been difficult to confide even in Lily. And she'd only done so because she'd felt she'd burst if she didn't unburden herself to someone.

Her family lamented the fact that she was such a loner and that she'd always gone her own way. Free-spirited was the kinder description they attributed to her. She was sure there were some less complimentary words they murmured to themselves. Flighty. Indecisive.

The simple fact was that even in a family as large and as loving as hers, a part of her always felt like she was on the outside. Even more so now that her brothers had done as her fathers and married the same woman.

And here she stood, the oddball. The one daughter in the midst.

"You asked me to back off before," Seth said when she

remained silent. "I respected your wishes, but you seem even sadder now. Can't you tell me what's going on?"

She winced at the subtle hurt in his voice. She forced a smile and then leaned up to brush a kiss across his cheek. "I love you, Seth. Don't push me. I'm dealing with this the best way I know how."

He didn't look happy. He looked like he wanted to shake her.

Then she frowned. "And don't go leaning on Lily for information. You'd put her in a terrible position. You know how loyal she is. She'd feel like she shouldn't keep anything from you and then it would upset her that she'd betrayed me."

Seth looked extremely disgruntled over how neatly Callie had prevented him from doing just that.

"You're a manipulative minx," he muttered.

She grinned cheekily. "You love me."

His expression grew serious and he reached out to cup her chin. "Yes I do love you, kiddo, and I hate to see you hurting. You know you can come to me with anything."

"You can't fix this for me, Seth. I know it goes against your every grain for me to say that because in your mind you'd do whatever it took. This is something I have to deal with on my own, and you know what? I can do it. I've been standing on my own two feet for years now."

He sighed. "Yeah. I'm proud of you, you know."

Her eyebrow went up.

He pulled her into a hug and she laid her head on his chest, soaking up the comfort her big brother always managed to give. Being home was the absolute best. The mountain was her haven. Her one safe place she could return to no matter how far she'd traveled. She loved the constancy of the land and her family.

"I am proud of you, Callie. You're an intelligent, independent young woman. All of us are proud of you."

"Don't make me cry or I'll wipe my nose on your shirt," she threatened.

He hastily stepped away and gazed warily at her. "So what are your plans for the day?"

"Honestly? I think I'm going up to see Mom and the dads. Grab a nap. I didn't sleep so well on the couch last night. I'll have dinner with them and spend the night there. It's been a while since I've had two consecutive nights off."

Seth frowned. "You're working too hard, Callie girl. There's no point. Dillon has plenty of employees."

She ignored him. "Are you all coming to lunch tomorrow? I'd love to take Lily riding down in the meadow. It's been a while since I was there."

Seth's gaze softened. He knew how special Callie's Meadow was to her. To all of them.

"Yeah, that sounds really good. I'm sure the others would love to come. It's been several days since I saw Mom or the dads. If we don't go, Mom will start squawking and then the dads will be all over our asses."

Callie chuckled. "Nice to see my big badass brothers are still cowed by a five-foot-nothing mama."

Seth didn't look at all embarrassed by that.

"Can I use your cell?" she suddenly asked. "Mine ran down."

Seth sighed and fished his phone out of his pocket. "For God's sake, Callie. How many times have I told you to keep track of your charger and more importantly charge your damn phone? What if something happens to you on the way up the mountain? Or you get stuck somewhere and have a dead cell phone?"

She tuned out the lecture because God did Seth love to get long-winded. It was what made him such a good cop. He could lecture anyone into submission.

She punched in her mom's number and shushed Seth with a finger over her lips as she waited for someone to pick up. A moment later, her father's voice filled her ear. She smiled. She couldn't help it. She might be twenty-three years old but she was still a total daddy's girl.

"Hi Dad," she said.

Ryan sighed. "Your phone dead again, Callie? Is that why you're using your brother's?"

She rolled her eyes. "Not you too. Seth is over here lecturing in my other ear."

"Someone needs to."

"Is Mom around? I wanted to ask her if she needed me to pick up anything in town. I was on my way over. I'm taking tonight off and thought I'd come to dinner and crash there if you guys don't mind."

"Of course we don't mind, Callie. This is your home. I miss my girl. You've been working too damn much. It's about time you took some time off. Hang on and let me ask your mother if she needs anything."

Some of the tightness in her chest eased as she waited for her dad to come back. Unconditional love was the sweetest gift anyone could offer. And in her family it abounded. Love and support were freely given. Never any strings. Unreserved. Fierce. Giving.

She wanted to wrap herself in her family's loving arms and never let go.

"Callie, your mom wants to know if you can run by and grab a grocery order. She's going to call it in so all you'll have to do is pick it up for her. She was planning to go into town today but this will save her a trip."

"Of course I will. Tell her I love her and I'll see her in an hour or so."

"She loves you too. I love you," he said gruffly.

"Love you too, Dad," she said with a catch in her voice. "See you later."

She handed the phone back to Seth who was back to watching her like she was some undiscovered specimen under a microscope.

"I've got to run," she said. "Mom needs me to go by the store. I'll see you tomorrow for lunch."

She slipped past him before he could start in on his interrogation again. The others were still sitting at the table, not that they weren't done. If she had to guess, Seth had made them stay while he went in to talk to her.

She blew kisses at Michael and Dillon, and then she leaned over and hugged Lily. "Thank you," she whispered in Lily's ear.

Lily squeezed her. "You're welcome."

Callie straightened, sent her brothers a smile and then headed out to her car.

Chapter Four

Could it be called an actual coincidence if he'd spent the entire morning prowling the small town of Clyde in hopes of running into Callie then to finally spot her when she got out of her car at the local grocery store?

Max stared down the street, drinking in the sight of the woman he'd spent so many nights aching for. She was beautiful. Spirited. She haunted his nights—and his days. His fingers tingled from the remembrance of her silky skin beneath his palm.

He'd had her in every conceivable way there was for a man to have a woman. She'd trusted him. Wholly and irrevocably. Callie did nothing in halves. Whatever she did, she threw herself wholeheartedly into it without reserve.

He watched as she strode from her car toward the doors of the store. At least three people stopped her, and she responded with a ready smile and patience he knew she didn't possess. For Callie to stand still even for a moment was like trying to catch the wind. She simply had too much to do and see to be deterred from her goal.

He stood for a moment and weighed his options. He had plenty of ammunition, but the one variable was always Callie. He never knew quite what to expect. It was what he enjoyed most about her.

Finally he decided to wait by her car until she came out. She'd have her arms full—hopefully, though he'd have to be concerned with whether she threw the bags at him.

He'd never been able to punish her for her impetuousness. To do so would be to quell what made her so beautiful to him. For a little while, she'd been his. She'd submitted to him and given him the gift of her trust. Her love.

He wanted it back. He wanted her back. In his bed. In his arms. His to command. His to cherish. He simply couldn't fathom his existence without her.

Unlike Callie, he was infinitely patient and he never conceded defeat. There was no option for him but success.

He didn't have long to wait. He'd barely gotten over to lean against the door of her little SUV before she appeared carrying two bags of groceries.

She didn't see him, which was just as well. The further she was from him, the more avenues she had of escape. But the fact that she was so oblivious of her surroundings, even in a town as small as Clyde and as loved as she obviously was, angered him. Anyone could target her, and it would be easy to get close enough to rob or harm her. He wanted to shield her and protect her, even when it was himself who'd caused her pain.

As she drew nearer, his breath caught in his throat. There were deep shadows under her eyes, shadows that he knew without arrogance he'd caused. There was a troubled set to her mouth, a mouth he'd tasted over and over. And her beautiful blue eyes were clouded as if she were miles away and unaware of her surroundings. Well, that much was evident because she still hadn't seen him and it wasn't as if he were a small man.

"Callie."

Her name came out more gruffly than he would have liked. There was a hesitancy that irritated him, and he realized that she did that to him. She made him uncertain when he lived his life in control and with complete confidence.

She halted so abruptly one of the bags slipped from her grasp. Having anticipated just such a possibility, he was quick to catch it before it fell to the ground.

She stared unblinkingly at him, hurt crowding the depths of her blue eyes. "Move, please. I'd like to get into my truck."

He pressed his lips together. She wasn't going to make it easy. Okay, he knew that, but her refusal to even allow him to explain pissed him off.

"I'm not moving until you agree to hear me out."

Her eyes flashed and he braced himself for the storm. His body leapt to hungry attention. He was starved for her, an admission that pained him to make, but he was nothing if not honest with himself.

"You talk to me as if I owe you something." Her voice was husky and strained as if it took everything for her to maintain her composure.

"You owe me nothing, Callie. But I owe you something."

At that she cocked her head and emotion swamped her eyes. "Yes, Max, you did owe me something. Unfortunately, I'm no longer interested in collecting. Now move or I'll scream the streets down."

He straightened and his nostrils flared as he pushed into her space. His legendary patience was wearing thin. "Scream then, Callie. Get us both arrested. Maybe we'll share a cell. At least then you'd be forced to listen to me. Now me, I'd rather have our talk in private, but if you insist on our personal business being bandied about in public, then so be it."

Her eyes narrowed. "We don't have any personal business. Not anymore."

"The hell we don't."

Not caring if she hauled off and slugged him again—a distinct possibility—he wrapped his free hand around her slim nape and slammed his mouth down over hers.

The groceries were crushed between them. Hell, he didn't care if they were ruined. He'd buy her more. All he knew was that if he didn't kiss her, he was going to explode.

Her taste filled his senses. Sweet and spicy, the delectable combination that was Callie Colter. He ravaged her mouth. He wanted to devour her whole. He wanted to drag her back to his shitty hotel room and spend the next three days making love to her until they couldn't move.

At first she responded as hungrily as he did. Her mouth moved softly over his and she returned the brush of his tongue with a tentative one of her own. It was as if she was reacquainting herself with his taste. Well, he'd never forgotten hers. There was damn well nothing to reacquaint himself with. How could there be when he'd dreamed of nothing else for the last months?

Then the moment was broken and she yanked away from him, tears crowding her beautiful eyes. "Why, Max? Will you not be happy until you've stripped me of everything? Okay, you proved it. Obviously I still want you. We've established that I'm an idiot. Are you happy now? You couldn't leave me with any of my pride intact?"

He swore long and bitter and rubbed a hand over his hair. He wanted to hold her and soothe the hurt and the anger so prevalent in her voice. But now wasn't the time for gentleness. He'd never get close to her unless he muscled his way in.

She already thought him a bastard. It wasn't as if he could get any lower in her esteem.

He took a step back, lifting the remaining bag of groceries

from her arms. "On your way up to your parents'?"

Her gaze sharpened. "That's none of your damn business."

"I'll show up there, Callie," he said calmly. "You know I will. I don't bluff. You have a choice. Come somewhere where we can discuss things in private. Or I'll come to your parents' house and we can hash it out in front of everyone. Either way, you *will* listen to me."

Helpless fury flashed across her features, and her eyes darkened to a blue-black storm cloud. "You stay away from my family."

"Then come with me."

"I have to bring groceries to my mom. She needs them for dinner and I'm expected there. I told her I'd be there. I won't back out."

"No, I suppose you won't. You're very loyal to your word. You keep your promises, don't you, Callie?"

"At least one of us does," she said in a bitter voice.

"I'll wait. Bring your mother her groceries. You have two hours to return or I come to you. I'm at the hotel. Room 102."

Her lips stretched into a thin line. She raised a shaking hand to shove her hair behind her ear. He could see how frustrated and helpless she felt. He hated what it did to both of them. The last thing he wanted was to break her. But neither would he allow her to turn her back on him, even if it was what she thought he'd done to her.

It *was* what he had done to her.

He opened the passenger door of her SUV and put the groceries on the seat. She was still standing where he'd left her when he turned back. She looked tired and shaken. He started to run his hand over her hair, but tightened his fingers into a fist at his side.

"Be warned, Callie. If you don't show, I'll come after you. I don't give a damn who your brother is. I'm not leaving until we talk."

Knowing that if he didn't leave now, his rigid control would be shattered, he turned and strode down the street toward his hotel. Every instinct screamed at him to turn back, to hold her, to offer her all the gentleness he so wanted to give her. To tell her he was sorry for being such a bastard.

But she'd have none of that. She was angry and hurt, and she wanted nothing to do with him. If he wanted a chance—any chance—of ever getting her to listen to him, he'd have to strong-arm her into meeting him.

Then and only then could he afford to show all that was in his heart.

Chapter Five

Callie's pulse raced all the way up the mountain to her parents' cabin. She alternated from seething with anger to swallowing against the knot growing in her throat.

She had to get it together. Her mom would know immediately that something had upset her, and while they'd reluctantly backed off when Callie had first returned home, she knew that wouldn't last forever.

By the time she pulled into her parents' drive she had a semblance of her control back. Her hands no longer shook and her jaw had relaxed enough that the ache in her teeth had dissipated.

She checked her watch and realized she had at most an hour at her parents' before she had to return to town. Max didn't make idle threats. She knew he was telling the absolute truth. He'd come to her parents' and then all hell would break loose.

Never had she chafed at being under Max's dominance. But now his arrogance and confidence that she'd do as he commanded was like acid in her stomach.

Willingly submitting and being blackmailed were two different matters entirely.

She sat a moment in her car as she willed herself to contain her battered emotions. She pulled the visor down and checked her appearance in the mirror, and then, satisfied that she looked the best she could given the circumstances, she opened her car door and got out.

She was halfway up the walkway with the bags of groceries when the front door opened and Ethan Colter stepped onto the porch.

A genuine smile worked over her face when she saw his tall, lanky form that age hadn't diminished one bit. Aside from the touches of silver at his temples and the smattering layered into the dark brown, time had been very good to him and he'd only grown more handsome with age. Her mom always said that she hadn't thought it possible for her husbands to get more lethal than they were when she met them but they'd proved her wrong.

"Hi Dad," she called.

He went to meet her and pulled her into a tight hug around the bags.

"Hi baby girl." He pressed a kiss to her temple and then drew away, taking the bags with him.

They mounted the steps together and went inside. As she always did whether it had been one day or months since she'd last been home, she inhaled deeply and allowed the scent of home and comfort to surround her in its warm embrace.

Adam was in the kitchen when she and Ethan trekked in, and his face lit up into a smile when he caught sight of Callie. He opened his arms and she walked into his hug.

"Hey baby girl," he said, echoing Ethan's endearment. It was what she'd been called for as long as she could remember and it always brought a smile to her face.

"Hi Dad. Where's Mom and Ryan?"

"Your mother is in her bedroom. I'll call her. Ryan's

probably with her," he added dryly.

Callie suppressed a chuckle at the implication. Her parents were still so in love that it made her ache, and they evidently still enjoyed an extremely healthy sex life. Not that she wanted to dwell on that, but it warmed her heart that after so many years her mom still had her husbands solidly wrapped around her little finger.

"So how have you been?" Ethan asked as he started putting away the groceries. "We haven't seen much of you lately."

There was gentle reproach in his voice and she sighed. Sadness and relief warred with each other. Relief that she was home where she felt safe and loved. Sadness that she had put such a distance between her and the people who loved her most in the world.

She stared at two of her fathers and felt something loosen inside. "Have I told you how glad I am to be home?"

They both turned to look at her and love shone in their weathered expressions. Ethan came to stand beside where she sat on the barstool and wrapped an arm around her shoulders. He squeezed and she leaned her head against his shoulder.

"We're glad you're home too. We always miss you when you're gone, and we worry."

She chuckled. "When don't you worry?"

Adam glared at her. "It's a father's prerogative to worry about his only daughter."

"Callie!"

Callie turned to see her mom burst into the room like a whirlwind. Her face was alight with a delighted smile as she closed in on her daughter.

Ethan relinquished her and Holly Colter enveloped Callie in a hug. Callie sighed with delight and let her mother cluck and pat and love on her. There really wasn't a better feeling.

When Holly finally let go, Callie looked up and saw Ryan leaning on the doorframe of the kitchen, a satisfied smile on his face. "It's always nice to see both my girls in the same room."

"Thanks for picking up the groceries," Holly said as she walked around the bar. "Not that I'll have much use for them, but your fathers will need the stuff to make dinner tonight."

Adam chuckled and shook his head. Holly's cooking skill, or lack thereof, was a family legend. It was generally accepted that she was encouraged to stay as far away from a stove as possible. Which was fine with her husbands, because there was nothing they liked better than pampering her shamelessly. A habit they'd continued with their only daughter.

Callie wasn't ashamed of the fact that she was hopelessly spoiled by her fathers. And to a degree, by her brothers as well.

"What time would you ladies like to eat?" Ethan asked.

Callie hesitated and dread tightened her throat. For just a minute she'd been able to put Max and her inevitable meeting with him from her mind.

"I know I said I was coming for dinner but I won't be able to stay after all," Callie said softly.

Her mom turned sharply, a frown creasing her pretty features. "Why not?"

"I totally forgot I told a friend of mine I'd meet them in town tonight. But I'll come home afterward. Seth said they were all coming for lunch tomorrow and I don't want to miss it."

She noticed the look that flowed between her dads but she didn't react.

Her mom checked her watch and then said, "You better be running along then. I worry when you're on the mountain roads late at night. Try not to be too late."

"Is your phone charging?" Ryan asked with mild exasperation.

Callie nodded. "It's charging in my truck now."

She rose from her stool and locked her knees to keep them from shaking. She hated that Max had made her so unsure of herself. What she really wanted to do was get this over with so she could move on and get over him. What she needed was a hot date. Unfortunately, there was a shortage of hot guys around Clyde, and the few that existed were either already attached or Callie had grown up with them.

"Love you guys. I'll see you later."

"Love you too, baby girl," Ethan called softly as she walked toward the front door.

She brooded the entire way into town. Then as she drove into the parking lot of the small motel, realization struck her. Maybe a little too hard.

She needed this face-to-face with Max. She needed closure. Seeing him hurt. A lot. A damn lot. But with the way they'd parted, seeing him again was the only way she was going to truly get over him.

Feeling marginally better, she steeled herself, took a deep breath and strode from her truck to Max's room and knocked crisply on the door.

She had but a moment to wait. Max opened the door and stood holding the edge, his gaze stroking up and down her body like he was memorizing her—or reacquainting himself with her.

Some of her courage died when she realized the close quarters they would be conducting their conversation in.

"Come in," he said quietly.

She shook her head and his eyebrow went up in surprise. No, he wasn't used to her saying no. When had she refused him anything?

The ache was back in her throat and she swallowed desperately against it.

"I think we should go somewhere public."

"You want what we have to say aired in front of others?"

"We can be in public and still have a private place," she said with a frown.

His hand tightened on the wood of the door and he cursed under his breath. "Do you think I'd hurt you? Do you honest to God think I'd ever hurt you?"

She shrugged. "You've already hurt me."

His breath hissed through his lips, and she saw some of his composure slip as fury brewed in his eyes. "Physically, Callie. Physically."

She wouldn't lie. "No. I don't think you'd hurt me. That's not what this is about. I just don't think a hotel room is the best place for us to talk about anything."

His eyes narrowed and then gleamed with quick understanding. "It isn't me you're afraid of, is it? It's yourself."

"Leave me my pride, at least," she whispered. "When have I ever been able to resist you? You know it. I know it. There's no reason for you to be so smug about it."

"Goddamn it," he swore. He swung the door open and gestured inside. "I won't touch you if you don't want me to. You have my word on that. It's your pride I'm trying to salvage by having this conversation in private. I don't really give a damn if people know how I feel about you. But I'd never humiliate you by airing our business in public."

Feeling chastened, she stepped inside his room and edged

over toward the one chair by the desk. She didn't want to be anywhere near his bed. It was unmade and the indention from where he'd slept was still outlined in the mattress and on the pillow. She'd bet anything his scent still lingered.

He sat on the edge and faced her, his eyes still glittering. For a long moment he simply stared at her. Then shadows crept over his face. "I've missed you."

She flinched and turned her face away, determined not to break down in front of him.

"Look at me, Callie."

The soft command in his voice was her undoing. It brought back too many nights where he'd commanded her over and over. She turned back to see answering grief in his eyes and it left her feeling unsettled.

"I need to explain why I left you in Greece."

She sucked in her breath and waited silently. It didn't really matter why he left. What mattered was why he'd never come back. Why he hadn't called. Why he'd done nothing to make her think any differently than he'd dumped her flat.

"My mother had been ill for quite some time. Even though she was ill, none of us expected her to have such a dramatic turn for the worse. She should have had years yet. She didn't."

Callie remained silent, unsure of what she was supposed to say. So she said nothing at all.

"My sister tracked me down in Greece. It was the first time I've ever purposely been out of contact with my family, or my business for that matter. I wanted nothing to intrude on my time with you.

"She told me I needed to come home…to say goodbye. My mother was dying and there wasn't a damn thing I could do about it. I went home and held my sister while our mother slipped away from us."

"I'm sorry," Callie said, not knowing what else to offer.

"I know I hurt you, Callie," he said quietly, pain echoing in his voice.

She curled her fingers into tight fists. "You couldn't tell me any of this *then*? What was so wrong with telling me why you had to go home? Did you think I wouldn't understand?"

He shook his head. "No, I never thought something so badly of you. I knew if I told you that you'd want to come with me."

His answer shocked her into silence and she stared at him as hurt crashed through her all over again.

"Damn it, Callie, don't look at me like that."

"Like what? Like it sounded like you had no desire for me to meet your family? What was wrong, Max? It's okay to fuck me all over Europe but heaven forbid your family is exposed to me?"

His eyes warned her she was going too far, but she continued on recklessly, her anguish blinding her to all else.

"I loved you, Max. I thought you loved me. Of course I would have wanted to go back with you. I would have wanted to be with you, to support you during such a horrible time. That's what love is all about."

She shuddered violently and clutched her arms over her chest as she hugged herself against so much hurt.

"I waited," she said painfully. "I waited for a month. I wouldn't go anywhere because I was afraid you'd come back and I'd be gone. I wouldn't let myself believe that you'd dumped me after all we shared. After I trusted you."

Max rubbed a hand over his face and closed his eyes.

"I finally had no choice but to leave because I was out of

money. You never called. You knew where I was and you never even so much as called to say what happened. To tell me you weren't coming."

"I was wrong," he said softly. "I was grief-stricken. My sister was inconsolable. We're the only family each other has. It took time to see to my mother's affairs. There were matters to settle. I had to ensure my sister's well-being. I knew I would never let you go. I knew that once I was able, I'd track you down no matter how long it took."

"Well, here I am," she said, spreading her arms, her hands palms-up. "As you can see, I'm fine. Your duty is done. You can leave now."

"You're not fine. Any fool can see that. You've lost weight. You have bruises under your eyes."

She shrugged. "I've moved on. I appreciate you coming all this way to let me know you didn't really mean to dump me and that you never gave me a thought during your haze of grief."

"That was cruel even given the circumstances," he bit out.

She raised her gaze to his and did nothing to shield her emotions from him. It wasn't like he couldn't see inside her. He'd always been able to see to the very heart of her.

"Cruel? If you loved me, Max, you would have at least sent a goddamn message. Five seconds. You can't tell me you couldn't tear yourself away from your sister and your mother's affairs for five seconds! I would have understood. I would have waited, no matter how long it took."

"I didn't want you to wait. I needed time to think!"

"Ah, now we get to the truth," she said scornfully. "You had cold feet. You jumped. I jumped. And it was too fast and you got scared."

His eyes blazed and anger rolled from him in waves. "You

don't have the market cornered on hurt, Callie. Yes, goddamn it. We moved way too fast. We burned each other up. I've never had a relationship that was as volatile and as passionate as ours. I worried I pushed you too hard, too far, too fast. You're young. I'm older than you. I needed time to sort a hell of a lot out, including us."

"Then you should have had the decency to at least tell me that over the phone," she said softly. "Because from where I stand, you took the coward's way out."

"Look at me and tell me you were certain about us. Tell me you had no doubts *and* that you were prepared to submit to me for the long-term."

She met his gaze and calm descended. She no longer shook. In a clear, steady voice, she said, "I had no doubts. I would have come back with you. I would have stayed. I would have done anything you wanted."

His eyes clouded and his hands curled and uncurled. He dragged a hand through his dark hair and she noted that his fingers shook. His reaction surprised her. He was always so cool and in control. He was a deeply passionate man, but not much shook him except the two of them when they came together. They were explosive, and yes, as he'd said, volatile.

"I made a mistake, Callie. But I'll be goddamned if both of us suffer the rest of our lives for it. I don't give a damn that you think you're over me or that you're moving on. I'm not over you and I'm damn sure not moving on."

He stared straight into her eyes, his face lined with ruthless determination. "Get used to seeing me, Callie. Because I'm not going anywhere until matters are settled between us. To my satisfaction. And to my satisfaction means you back in my bed where you damn well belong."

Chapter Six

"You honest to God think I'm going to fall back into bed with you just because you arrive with some legitimate excuse for breaking my heart? Yeah, it sounds ridiculous and cheesy. But the truth is you destroyed something inside me, Max. I'm not sure you're the one to fix it."

He pressed in close and grasped her shoulders in his strong hands. "I'm the only damn one who can fix it, Callie. Me. No one else. You gave yourself to me. Well, I'm not letting you take yourself back. You're mine. I won't let you go. I *can't* let you go."

She stared helplessly at him, unsure of what she was supposed to do or say. She was still angry. She wasn't ready to let go of that anger, because the alternative was more grief.

"You trusted me once," he said in frustration. "You'll trust me again. As long as it takes, you'll trust me."

Her eyes narrowed and she turned her head to the side. "What are you saying? Are you moving to Clyde? Taking up residence here? Because this is my home. This is my sanctuary, my refuge. I don't want you here."

He pulled her in close until her body was flush against his and his heat seeped into her until he surrounded her like a blanket.

"*I* was your refuge. *I* was your sanctuary. I will be again. I'm staying here as long as it takes. I'm not shy. I have no problem going after something I want. Just be prepared to see me. A lot."

"You sound like a damn stalker," she said in disgust.

His nostrils flared in distaste. "Stalking, Callie? Really? Is that what you've lowered me to now? I'm here because I'm not letting you go. If that makes me a stalker then I'll have to deal. I'm just warning you. Plan to see a lot of me from now on."

With that, he grasped her nape and held her as his mouth closed over hers. It wasn't a gentle kiss a man might give his lover in apology. No, Max had already done what little groveling he planned to do. It wasn't in his nature to pull back. Never during sex. Never with kissing or touching. He was demanding and strong. Always pushing, testing those limits and pulling back at just the right time.

His taste burst into her mouth. She'd missed this. God, she missed him. His tongue stroked knowingly over hers, warm and slightly rough as he explored her tender mouth.

Her body came alive, responding instantly to his touch. Recognition of a lost mate.

He was a wall, hard, protecting, and her soft curves melted against him as he pulled her more firmly into his arms. No escape. He forced her to acknowledge him and the all-consuming passion between them.

Raw. Carnal. They'd always been a combustible force. It was one she didn't understand. The attraction between them bewildered her in its intensity. She'd been with other men. She'd kissed them. Flirted. Felt the easy flare of attraction. But with Max, she found herself powerless to deny the fire that burned between them.

Even worse than the tide of arousal unfurling deep within her was the fierce ache that bloomed in her heart and spread with frightening intensity. Grief. Regret. So much regret.

She slid her hands between them, intent on pushing him away, but the moment she felt the ripple of muscles across her fingers, her touch became seeking.

He fed delicately at her mouth. Demanding and yet tender. His tongue swept over her lips, as though he were determined to taste every part of her.

His grip tightened at her nape and he angled in sharper, holding her as he ran his other hand up her side to cup her breast. His thumb brushed across one sensitive peak through the thin material of her T-shirt and she went still.

She pushed hard and stumbled away, her knees shaking so badly it was a wonder she didn't go down. She wiped at her mouth with the back of her hand as if such a gesture could possibly erase his imprint.

Months of separation hadn't begun to erase his mark on her. One ineffectual wipe of her hand certainly wouldn't do it now.

"Look at me and tell me we're done," he bit out. "Look me in the eye, Callie. Tell me you want me gone. That you never want to see me again."

Tears flooded her eyes and she stood, so starkly vulnerable, so *wasted* before him.

He swore softly and moved toward her again. This time he carefully took her into his arms and simply hugged her to his tall frame. He pressed her head to his chest and held her there as he rubbed his hand up and down her back.

"I asked you to look at me," he whispered. "But never like that, Callie, love. Never like that, with so much hurt in your eyes that it makes my teeth ache. I put it there, I know, but give me a chance to take it away. It's all I'm asking. Give us a chance."

She closed her eyes and melted into him. He backed toward

the bed and sat, taking her with him, enfolding her in his embrace until she was curled onto his lap, her head tucked underneath his chin.

"I never meant to hurt you like this," he said in a tone loaded with self-derision. "I handled it badly. I handled us badly. And you're right. I did run. But I couldn't go far. You kept pulling me back. Always back to you."

She pulled her head away so she could look into his eyes. All she saw was a burning intensity. No deception. He didn't look away. "What do you want, Max?" she asked softly.

"Haven't you been listening? I want you."

She looked briefly away but then his fingers nudged at her chin and forced her to look back at him.

"For how long this time? What about when it's time for you to leave? Or the next emergency happens? Or you decide you're not cut out for a relationship? This is my home, Max. I'm not fucking around with you or indulging in some hot fling where my family lives. They're important to me. They're everything to me."

He sighed and brushed a strand of hair from her forehead. "I know I have a lot of ground to regain. Your trust has been damaged. I get that. But give me a chance, Callie. You and me. Let's do it right this time."

"Define right."

"I take you out to dinner. You take me to meet your family. We go out on dates. You show me your town. Show me the places you love. Show me what makes you *you*."

She sucked in a deep breath. Her heart was fluttering so madly that she had a hard time getting air in and out of her lungs.

"Okay," she said quietly.

"No, not okay, like you've just received a death sentence. Do it because you want me like I want you. Show me that woman I fell head over ass for. The woman who doesn't take shit off anyone. Who has so much fire she burns me with every touch. That's the woman I want back."

Her lips slid slowly upward into a smile.

"I missed you, Max."

He crushed her to him, and it was then she could feel that his heart was every bit as out of control as hers. It thudded against her skin like the wings of a hummingbird.

"I missed you too. So damn much. There was a hole in my chest that was eating me alive."

Hope fluttered up, tentative but there. It was tempting to squash it back down. She'd already been hurt so much. But more than the hurt, something came alive inside her, bubbled up until it overwhelmed her. Joy. It had been so long since she'd felt remotely happy that the sensation was alien.

"Tell me yes, Callie. Tell me you're in this thing with me."

She reached for him this time, the first time she'd made an overt gesture to touch him. She brushed her hands over his cheeks, felt the rasp of stubble on his jaw. Then she leaned in and kissed him softly.

"Yes."

He groaned but allowed her free rein. She could feel the tension flowing from his coiled muscles. How he remained so still when his very nature demanded that he dominate amazed her.

She pulled away, her fingers slowly falling from his face. He caught her hands and pulled them between them to rest against his stomach.

"There's just one other thing we need to come to an

understanding about."

She eyed him warily as his gaze roved possessively over her.

"We're together. In every sense of the word. Which means you in my bed. Every night. No matter what. I'm willing to do whatever it takes to build us again but that includes us in the bedroom as well."

She inhaled sharply, her body automatically responding to the dominance in his voice.

"The words. I want the words."

She licked her lips nervously and then slowly nodded. "All right."

Chapter Seven

Callie stumbled from Max's hotel room, her mind and senses reeling. He hadn't wanted her to go. He'd wanted her to stay with him. But she needed time to process what had just happened. And her parents were expecting her. Lunch tomorrow. She'd told them she'd be back tonight.

She hadn't invited Max. Maybe that hurt him. But she simply wasn't ready to introduce him to her family. She first had to come to terms with and resolve herself to the abrupt change that was her relationship with Max.

How could she go from deeply wounded to suddenly happy? Her family would smell a rat a mile away. Then they'd want an explanation, and she wasn't ready to spill what had transpired between her and Max.

They would be angry. Understandably so, and their relationship with Max would forever be tarnished by the fact he'd hurt her so badly. They wouldn't forgive so easily.

She got into her SUV and drove. No direction. No clear destination. She circled the small town and pulled up to the bar. Dillon would be working tonight since he'd ordered her to take the night off. Which meant that Lily was home with only Michael and Seth.

She'd promised her mom she'd be back, but she couldn't go yet. Not without talking to Lily. Her mind was about to explode and she needed to unload. Lily was the only person who knew the whole story.

She backed out of the parking lot and turned in the direction of Dillon's cabin. It wasn't a far drive from town, but it was down a winding private road that dead-ended at his house.

Her hands shook on the steering wheel, and she took her time, not trusting herself not to wind up in a ditch. When she finally pulled up to the cabin, she breathed a sigh of relief and shut off the engine.

Before she was fully out of her truck, Seth appeared on the front porch and leaned against one of the posts, his gaze sharp as he watched her get out.

She smiled or at least she thought she did. Her entire face felt frozen and her lips were still swollen from Max's kisses.

"I thought you were staying with Mom and the dads tonight."

"I was. I am. I had to meet a friend in town. I'd totally forgotten. I told Mom I'd be up later."

The lie fell clumsily from her lips and she hated it. She never lied to her family. She never held anything back from them. Until now. Until Max.

Seth pushed off the post and held out his arms. She went into his embrace and hugged him tightly. As she pulled away, she glanced up at him. "What was that for?"

"You looked like you needed it."

It was all she could do to hold the tears at bay. She bit her lip and tried to gather her scrambled senses.

"Is Lily busy? I wanted to see her."

If he thought it was nuts that she was back to see Lily again, he didn't comment.

"She's never too busy to see you. She's inside. Go on in."

Callie pushed open the door, leaving Seth on the porch. Lily was on the couch, her feet in Michael's lap while they watched a movie. When they looked up and saw Callie, Lily swung her feet to the floor and sat up.

"Callie! I thought you were up at your parents'. Is everything okay?"

Callie smiled. "I'm going later." She glanced over at Michael who suddenly stood and took a step toward the door.

"I'm just going out to see if Seth needs any…help."

Grateful that both her brothers had taken the hint, Callie plopped onto the couch beside Lily who was looking at her with deep concern in her eyes.

"It's him, isn't it?" Lily said in a low voice. "Max. He's upset you again. I really think we should tell Seth so he can get rid of him."

Callie leaned her head back against the couch and closed her eyes. "Oh Lord, Lily, I don't know what to think."

Lily scooted closer on the couch until her knee was touching Callie's thigh. "What happened?"

Callie opened her eyes and turned her head in Lily's direction. "I saw him after I left here this morning. Outside the grocery store. He insisted I see him. He wanted to talk. He threatened to show up at Mom and Dads' if he had to."

Lily's mouth dropped open. "He can't do that! He can't get away with threatening you. I'd like to see him try to show up at your parents' house. Your dads would kick his ass and if there was anything left, Seth, Michael and Dillon would finish the job."

Callie held up her hand. "He wasn't threatening, like menacing or anything. He wouldn't hurt me. God, I've made him sound like a deranged stalker or something. It's complicated. I told him I'd meet him at his hotel room after I dropped off Mom's groceries. I made excuses to Mom and the dads about why I couldn't stay for supper."

"Oh Callie." Lily's mouth turned down into a sympathetic moue. "Tell me you didn't go see him."

"I did."

"And?"

Callie sighed and rubbed a hand through her hair. God, she was tired and emotionally spent.

"He wants to get back together."

"Over my dead body!" Lily said fiercely. "Did you tell him that ship had already sailed?"

Knowing Lily needed the entire sordid tale, Callie recounted everything Max had said in the hotel room. From start to finish. When she was done, Lily sat back, a pensive frown on her face.

"Am I making it too easy?" Callie asked. "I don't know what to do. I love him. I still love him. But am I falling back into his arms too easily? I mean, the reasons why he left are valid. But the way he handled the entire situation is just twisted. What if I let him back in and he does it all over again?"

"Does he love you?" Lily asked quietly.

Callie heaved out another sigh. "That's the question, isn't it? I'm not desperate enough to ask. Maybe I'm too prideful, but I won't set myself up for that kind of rejection. I know he cares about me. Call me stupid, but he can't fake that kind of reaction. He was sincere. Angry and frustrated and sincere. Anytime we're together it's like dry wood to a flame. We both go up. If he didn't care, then why go to all this trouble? Why not just let go? I mean, he made the break. It was done. He never had to see me again. I certainly wouldn't know how to find him."

"Those are good questions," Lily murmured.

"I feel like an idiot. I mean, I come home and mope around for months, and the minute he walks into town I'm supposed to just forget how much I've hurt all this time and take him back?"

"Well, no."

"But on the other hand, does it make me a petty bitch to want him to suffer and to tell him no, no, no, until I feel like he's paid his penance and then let him crawl back into my life? How does that make *me* any happier?"

"It doesn't," Lily said softly. "Honey, listen to me. All you need to consider is what makes you happy. Stop worrying about what you think you should do to save face or pride or whatever it is you think you need to do. Those things won't matter in the end. The real question you need to be asking yourself is whether you trust him and whether you're willing to take a chance on him again. He hurt you. It isn't about punishing him or yourself. It needs to be about what you want and what you're willing to forgive."

Callie stared at her sister-in-law and then leaned forward to hug her fiercely. "I love you, you know. I'm so glad I have you."

Lily laughed and squeezed Callie in return. They hung onto each other for a long moment before Callie finally pulled away.

"I guess maybe I want him to suffer as much as I have so he'll realize how badly he hurt me."

"Who says he hasn't? From all you've told me, he's not been any happier than you have, and he had to deal with the loss of his mother on top of all that. I'm not saying he didn't deserve to be miserable for the way he treated you, but maybe you aren't the only one who has suffered."

"You're a wise woman, Lily Colter. I know I'm being petty."

Lily squeezed her hand. "No, hon, you're a woman who's been hurt by the man she loves."

"I don't know what I'm supposed to do next," Callie admitted. "He wants to pick up where we left off. He wants me in his bed every night. I'm not sure we can overcome the separation between us that quickly."

"He may want, but that doesn't mean he'll get," Lily said lightly.

"Oh Max always gets what he wants," Callie said in resignation. "I have no willpower where that man is concerned. He's lethal."

Lily's eyebrows rose. "That good, huh?"

"Uh-huh."

Lily laughed. "Callie, I've never known you to back down from anyone or anything. Granted our acquaintance is still somewhat new, but your brothers have regaled me with tales of your childhood and your adulthood as well. If anyone can stand up to this Max, I'd say it would be you."

"Think Mom would kill me if I didn't make it back up the mountain tonight?"

"Tell you what. I'll call her and tell her I asked you to stay over. Then we can all ride up together tomorrow for lunch."

"You are way too good to me, Lily, but I love you dearly for it."

Lily touched her arm and her expression went serious. "You once helped me through one of the most difficult days of my life, Callie. I'd say we're good for each other."

"We girls have to stick together," Callie said solemnly. "In this family, we're way outnumbered!"

Chapter Eight

The next morning, Callie was still sleeping soundly when Lily gently shook her awake. Callie blinked fuzzily and let out a groan. "Is it morning already?"

Lily smiled. "Yeah. I wouldn't let the guys wake you and made them tiptoe through the living room. They're going ahead. I told them I'd ride up with you. That'll give you time to shower and feel human before you face the entire family."

Callie reached up, framed Lily's face and then smacked her noisily on the forehead. "God, I love you."

She heaved herself up and planted her feet on the floor. "What time is it anyway?"

"Eleven. You'll need to hurry if we're going to make lunch."

Callie pushed herself up and staggered toward the bathroom. Twenty minutes later, feeling somewhat human again, she came back into the living room where Lily was sitting in the armchair.

"Ready?" Lily asked.

Callie nodded.

Lily looked dubiously at Callie. "Want me to drive?"

"No, I'm okay."

"Did you sleep at all last night?" Lily asked once they started down the road toward town.

Callie grimaced. "Not much, I'll admit. Thinking too much."

"Did you come to any groundbreaking conclusions?"

"Just that Max has a hold on me that months of separation and anger haven't managed to break," she said bleakly.

"You don't sound happy about that."

Callie's hands tightened around the steering wheel. She held her breath as she turned down Main Street and drove past the hotel where Max was staying. Only when they were beyond did she acknowledge Lily's statement.

"There's a part of me that's happy. Really, really happy. Like that bubbly, giddy feeling you get when you're really excited about something."

"And the other part?"

"Like I'm worried I'm standing on railroad tracks with a freight train bearing down on me."

"Well, that's an image," Lily muttered.

Callie chuckled. "Best I could come up with on such short notice, but it fits."

They drove in silence for a few moments longer. Callie turned onto the road that led up the mountain to her parents' house and deftly navigated the holes, the switchbacks and the loose dirt.

"It's my pride," she finally admitted. "I can't get beyond my pride. It sounds so stupid. I feel stupid."

"It's not stupid, Callie. Pride is important." Lily reached over and squeezed Callie's knee. "It's going to be okay. Just remember you don't have to be pressured into anything you don't want. This is your turf. He has to come to you. You aren't at a disadvantage here. He is."

Callie smiled and rounded the corner to the turnoff for her parents' cabin. She shot between the tall pines and rolled to a stop behind Seth's truck. Then she checked her watch. "Made it with fifteen minutes to spare. Now Mom won't gripe because the food got cold."

"Like she'd know." Lily snorted. "Your dads are the ones getting the food on the table."

Callie broke into laughter. "Yeah, so true."

The both got out and hurried up the steps. Callie opened the door, stuck her head in and yelled, "We're here!"

To her surprise, when she walked in, her parents—all four of them—and her brothers were sitting in the living room, their faces set in determination. And they were all staring at her.

"Uh-oh," Callie murmured to Lily.

Lily shot her a look of apology and turned her palms up as if to say she had no idea what was up. Callie let out a small groan. D-day. The day her family was no longer going to be put off.

She knew those looks. Saw the worry in her mom's eyes. Saw the grim set of her fathers' and brothers' lips. Yeah, she was going to get it from all sides. She was tempted to turn around and run like hell, but she wasn't a coward.

She took a step forward and wiped her palms down her jeans. "Hey guys."

"Callie, come sit down," Adam said in a low voice.

She winced. It was that tone that brooked no arguments. Even at twenty-three years old she wasn't too old to heed her dad's order. He didn't give them very often, but when he did, he meant business.

With a sigh, she flopped onto the couch next to Seth. Seth was her ally. Always had been. Only now he didn't look like much of an ally. He looked as determined as her other family members to make her talk.

Ryan leaned forward, resting his forearms on his legs. He stared at her with those blue eyes so like her own. "What's going on, baby girl? Don't you think it's time you told us what's wrong?"

"You've been moping around here for months now," Ethan cut in. "You came home like a wounded animal and I don't see that it's gotten any better."

Tears pricked her eyelids, and the people she loved so dearly went bleary in front of her. Lily came to stand beside her and put a soft hand on her shoulder in support.

"Callie, we're worried," her mom said. "You just aren't yourself."

She scrubbed a hand over her face and heaved another sigh of resignation. "I met someone while I was in Europe."

Adam got this pinched look on his face like he did when he wanted to kick someone's ass. Lord but this wasn't the way she wanted to introduce Max to her family.

"His name is Max. We had a...misunderstanding."

Seth snorted beside her. "What kind of misunderstanding? Is it the type of misunderstanding that I need to track the son of a bitch down and kill him?"

She twisted her hands nervously in her lap and peeked back up at her fathers. "He's here. In Clyde, I mean."

You could have broken a brick on their faces. Ethan's eyes narrowed and Ryan scowled.

She held up a hand. "I want you to meet him."

"Maybe you need to explain this misunderstanding first," Adam said.

Holly got up from her position between Ryan and Ethan and moved over to where Callie sat. With a flick of her hand, she motioned Seth from his seat and then settled next to her daughter.

"What happened, baby?"

Oh Lord but she wished her mother had stayed across the room. Callie's lips trembled and her nose drew up and stung as tears burned her eyes.

It was all over with the moment her mom pulled her into her arms. She buried her head against her mother's chest and allowed some of her misery to pour out.

Holly rocked her back and forth and stroked a hand through Callie's hair. Several long moments later, Callie gained control of herself and immediately felt like an idiot.

"God," she groaned against her mom. "Make them go away, Mom. This is humiliating."

Holly chuckled. "I'm afraid you're stuck with them."

"Lily can stay," Callie said mournfully.

"Callie."

Ryan's voice reached her ears. It was a soft command. Full of love. She looked up, unable to deny her father.

"If you really want us to go, we will. We love you. It's been hard watching you hurt and not being able to do a damn thing about it. We only want to help."

Callie smiled and wiped at the damp trails on her cheeks. "I don't want you to hate him."

"I can't promise to like him if he hurt my baby," Ryan said evenly.

"He wants us to be together," she said.

"And what do you want?" Adam asked.

She drew in a deep breath. "I want us to be together too. If I can forgive him, I want you to be able to forgive him too."

Holly squeezed Callie's hand. "I'm sure we'll love him." She shot a challenging look in her husbands' direction. "We have to meet him first, of course. And I have to be sure he's someone I can trust my daughter with."

The sharpness in Holly's tone made her sons snicker. She silenced them with a look.

"Did Max have anything to do with what happened the other night at the bar?" Dillon asked.

Callie shot him a glare. "Who told you?"

Dillon stared balefully at her. "It's my bar, Callie. Did you think no one would say anything?"

She scowled and pressed her lips together.

Her fathers' collective sigh echoed in the room.

"It was nothing," she said defensively. "I might have hit Max when he showed up at the bar. I wasn't expecting him. I was pissed."

"How do you maybe hit someone?" Michael drawled.

"Okay, so I decked him. At the time he deserved it."

"And yet you're ready to be with this guy again," Adam said with a scowl.

"Look Dad, it's complicated. He had to leave Europe because his mom was dying. I thought he dumped me." She left out the part where he'd done just that for all practical purposes. It wouldn't put him in a very good light with her already skeptical parents. "He found me here. He apologized." Or as much as Max was capable of apology. More like he demanded she forgive him. Which wasn't the same thing at all. "He wants...me."

Ethan sighed. "We'll give him a chance, Callie. What do you know about this guy, anyway? What does he do? He's not planning to take you away from here, is he?"

At that statement, she got scowls from her dads and her

brothers. Even Holly frowned and looked at Callie in question.

"I…" Hell. It made her sound ridiculously stupid, but the truth was, she didn't know a whole lot about what Max did. She knew he was wealthy. She knew he had a job. Or maybe it was that he owned his own business. Finance? Truth be told, she hadn't cared whether he had money. She hadn't cared what his job title was.

"Callie?" Adam prompted.

"He's in finance," she mumbled.

"I think we should meet him before we make judgment," Lily said in her sweet, soft voice. "We shouldn't make Callie feel worse than she already does. She's been through a lot. Our support means a lot to her."

Oh damn. Callie was going to cry again. She looked up and smiled gratefully at Lily who still stood beside the couch where Callie sat.

Ryan cleared his throat. "Invite him to dinner. The sooner the better."

"Just don't make it the Spanish Inquisition," Callie muttered. "It's bad enough there are so many damn males in this family. Dial down the testosterone for the evening if you don't mind."

Dillon snickered and she glowered at him.

"I'll have your fathers make something special," Holly said serenely. "If it turns out we don't like him, I'll cook the next meal for him."

The entire room erupted in laughter.

Some of the tension in Callie's chest loosened, and she grinned at the mischievous glint in her mom's eyes. Holly patted Callie on the leg.

"It's going to be fine," she whispered. "You'll see. Your

fathers are growly, but you're their baby. You have to remember that."

"Yeah, I know," Callie returned. "I love you, Mom."

"I love you too, sweetheart."

Holly enfolded her into another hug and when she released her, Adam rose from the couch. "Now that we have that out of the way, are you all ready to eat?"

And then Callie was surrounded by her fathers, all hugging her and being gruff, and for the first time since she'd returned home months before, she felt a lightness slide through her soul that told her everything just might be all right.

Chapter Nine

Callie parked in front of Max's hotel and sat there for a long moment staring out her windshield. She was exhausted from the afternoon at her parents' but her senses were alive at the thought of seeing Max again. This time without the hurt and misunderstanding of the past between them.

Could they really start over so easily? Could she?

She opened her car door and stepped out, wiping her hands nervously down her jeans. Her stomach fluttered and her chest tightened with each step she took toward the door to Max's room.

She raised her hand to knock and froze before quietly resting her hand against the aged wood. She was considering backing away when the door suddenly opened, and her hand fell.

"Callie."

She took a step back and knotted her fingers together in front of her. "Max."

He arched an eyebrow. "Were you going to knock or were you going to stand there all evening?"

"How did you..."

"I saw you pull up. I've been waiting for you."

When she didn't immediately make a move, he stood back

and opened the door wider. "Come in."

She took a deep breath and stepped into the lion's den. Or at least it felt like it. The door closed behind her and she stopped in the middle of the hotel room.

Firm hands slid up her arms to grasp her shoulders and then warm, sensual lips pressed to the curve of her neck. She shivered and closed her eyes as sweet pleasure hummed through her veins. A welcome song.

"You smell just as I remember," he murmured. "Sweet and a little exotic. Like wild honeysuckle in bloom." He swept his tongue up to the hollow behind her ear. "And you taste every bit as sweet as you smell."

"Max," she whispered.

Slowly he turned her, his hands never leaving her arms. He stepped in closer until she was pressed to his chest. Then he moved his hands up to cup her face and he lowered his head to kiss her.

A moan gathered low in her throat, swelled and then slipped past her lips into his mouth. He ate delicately at her lips, nipping then sucking, and then he traced a line with his tongue before plunging deep.

There was nothing tentative or seeking about his kiss. He exerted the same mastery that had attracted her to him in the first place. Strong. Determined. And possessive. So very possessive.

He kissed her mouth and then pressed a tender line down one side of her jaw then up to her temple before skipping over to the other side to repeat all over again. He kissed her forehead and then pressed his mouth to her hairline and let it linger.

Tension coiled tight in his muscles. Whispered through his body and into hers until they were two wound springs.

When he finally pulled away, his fingers threaded through her hair, stroking absently as though he couldn't keep from touching her.

"I'm going to make love to you, Callie. I can hardly think straight for wanting you. And God, I don't think I can be easy. You deserve easy. Gentle and loving. You deserve for me to handle you like a piece of delicate glass. I don't think I can."

His words, so hoarse, his need so prevalent was like warm sunlight after a long winter. She stared up at him then touched his face with trembling fingers. "Then don't be," she whispered. "Just love me."

With a harsh groan he yanked her into his arms. She hit his chest with enough force to knock the breath from her, and his mouth devoured her all over again.

He walked her backwards even as he yanked at her shirt, pulling it from her jeans. He shoved impatiently, freeing her from the shirt, and he wasted no time going for her pants. With one hand, he fumbled with her snap while with the other he unclasped her bra.

With her jeans still snagged at her knees, he tumbled her onto the bed. He tugged at her jeans until they came away, and the denim went sailing across the room to hit the door with a thud.

Then he set to work on his own clothing and she lay there, staring through half-lidded eyes as he revealed his muscular, tanned body.

He was leaner. A little thinner than he'd been before. The whorl of dark hair at the hollow of his chest tapered to a dark line below his navel where it disappeared into the band of his slacks.

Some of his impatience eased when he saw her watching him. He paused at his fly and began a slow tease that left her breathless with anticipation.

Inch by delicious inch, he peeled the material down his body until the dark hair at his groin became visible and then his cock slid out, distended and swollen.

When he was finally nude, he crawled onto the bed and straddled her body as he stared down as if memorizing every inch of her all over again.

"You're so beautiful. So perfect. Perfect for me. Just the right amount of soft and sweet with a thread of steel at your very core. I don't think a more perfect woman was ever made."

Her breath caught and hiccupped out until her throat burned with emotion. He'd always been able to say the right thing. He didn't throw words out carelessly. Everything he ever had to say was measured and weighed. And so exquisitely rendered.

He was a man who when he talked, others listened. There was something in his tone that commanded respect. And obedience.

"Do you want me, Callie? Do you want me like I want you?"

She swallowed and nodded.

"The words. I want the words."

"Yes, I want you, Max," she said in a low voice.

"Put your arms over your head."

She raised her hands and leaned back until her arms were high above her head and her knuckles grazed the edge of the mattress.

Slowly he backed away from her and off the bed until he stood between her thighs. Then he slid his fingers up her legs to hook into the waistband of her lacy underwear.

He tugged gently, and the tiny scrap eased over her pussy and down her legs to her knees. Her legs trembled as he pulled her underwear the rest of the way off and she was naked and vulnerable to his gaze.

"Spread your legs for me," he said. "I want to see you again. I want to taste you."

She was barely able to comply, her knees shook so badly. She knew she was wet for him. Knew she wanted him so much. His touch. His tongue. His mouth. Everything. It had been so long. So very long.

Her heart and her body ached for him.

He leaned down and carefully thumbed through her folds, testing her softness. He dipped a finger into her opening and slid it upward, making her flesh slick with her desire.

He traced a circle around her clit until she squirmed and lifted her hips, wanting more.

"Keep your arms above you," he reminded her when she would have lowered her hands to reach for him. "Or I'll have to tie them."

Oh God. Memories of her bound and completely at his mercy exploded through her mind. He'd tied her hands. He'd tied her legs. He'd had her complete submission. And he'd owned her body and soul over and over and over...

He lowered his head even as he parted her with his fingers. Warm air blew over her sensitive flesh as his breath huffed out just before his tongue touched her opening.

She strained upward only to be issued a sharp reprimand to be still. She panted, her chest heaving as she fought for control. It had simply been too long. She couldn't possibly restrain herself. She couldn't do his bidding when her body screamed for him.

"Please," she begged. "I need you."

He glanced up at her, his green eyes smoldering so hot she

shivered. "Do you want it rough? Do you want me to take you now before you're ready?"

"I'm ready," she gasped out. "Please, Max."

His hands curled around her knees, and he yanked her down until her ass rode the edge of the mattress. He spread her, positioned his cock and thrust forward.

His entry was a shock. No matter that she thought she was ready, he was big and swollen and it had been a long time for her. Her body hugged him so tight she wondered if it was even possible for him to go deeper.

He withdrew and then hammered forward, opening her ruthlessly with the force of his thrust. All the while his gaze was fastened on her. His eyes glittered. Wild. So unlike his usual controlled, cool stare.

His face was drawn with harsh lines. His lips were thin and flat, and his nostrils flared even as he powered into her again. Her body shuddered. She felt small and helpless, prisoner to the pleasure he took from her body.

She closed her eyes in bliss as her pussy rippled around his cock. She arched her body, stretching, welcoming him back.

"Open your eyes, Callie. Look at me. Only at me."

Her eyelids fluttered and she did as he directed.

His lips twisted savagely as he grasped her hips, opened her wider and forced himself deeper. He thrust so hard against her that her body shook. Her breasts jiggled with each movement, and the sharp slap of his groin against her ass sent a jolt of pleasure, razor sharp, through her belly.

He leaned over her, pinning her body to the mattress as his body powered over hers. In and out. Rougher, harder until she bit her bottom lip from the exquisite, overwhelming sensations bombarding her at every turn.

She wouldn't last. Couldn't. Not against his onslaught. Not after so long.

Pressure built, coiled in her belly and tightened every one of her muscles until she was weak from the strain. Her nipples beaded and puckered, and a thousand tiny chill bumps raced over her skin as the flames of her orgasm fanned higher and higher.

He was so big and she was so tight. She felt him in every part of her body, sliding like velvet through her most delicate tissues.

Not once did he pause. He pushed. Harder and harder. Relentless. His jaw bulged and he stared down at her, his gaze flashing over her face.

"Come."

The quiet order was like a short fuse. It whipped over her body and unlocked something deep within her soul. Her release flashed like lightning. She let out a sharp cry and she came apart, piece by jagged piece.

Her vision dimmed. He and the room blurred but through it all she stayed locked on him. He'd demand no less. He was her anchor. Her shelter. Her strength. Her very soul.

He fell on her, gathering her into his arms as his hips rocked spasmodically against her. She felt the quick wetness between her legs, and the ease with which he slid into her body now.

For a long moment he lay over her body, blanketing her protectively, his chest pushing into hers as he sought to catch his breath.

Their legs were tangled, and he rubbed one hair-roughened limb up and down her thigh before he finally rolled to his side, taking her with him.

He pulled out of her in a warm rush of semen and then he pressed his lips to her forehead.

She stiffened and he went still. Her pulse bounded even as his hand came up to rub up and down her arm.

"Callie?" he asked in a low voice. "What's wrong? Did I hurt you?"

She rolled to her back and stared up at the ceiling as realization crashed through the euphoric haze surrounding them. He let her go, surprising her, even though he rose up on one elbow to look at her through narrowed eyes.

"You didn't use a condom."

She rolled away from him and curled her legs to her belly, wishing desperately she had covers to pull over her.

He touched her arm but she didn't acknowledge the touch even though she knew it was a command for her to look at him.

"We didn't use condoms before. I saw no use for them now."

"That was before."

"Before what, Callie?"

She exhaled long and slow. "That was months ago. You weren't with anyone else. I don't know who you've been with since. It's not fair to me. Nor is it safe. You should have used one."

This time he didn't ask. He simply rolled her over until she was forced to meet his angry gaze. "You think I was with other women after I left you?"

She lifted one shoulder in a shrug. "I don't know. That's the point. You should have used protection until we could talk about it."

He swore under his breath. "There's been no one else. Not since you."

She stared for a long time, judging the veracity of his

words. She hated that there was doubt. Before she would have embraced his words. She hadn't believed him capable of lying to her. He wasn't a man who lied. But in a way he had. He'd told her he wanted to be with her. And he'd left her.

He spread her legs, and to her shock she felt him prodding at her with his cock, hard and erect again. He slid deep, his semen making his entry easy this time. He was deep and hard inside her, and he stared down at her, his face stormy as he pushed into her again.

"Just you, Callie. You haunted my nights. My days. I never stopped thinking about you. How could I possibly go to bed with another woman who wasn't you?"

Her mouth rounded in shock as he thrust deep and hard through her swollen tissues.

She was so hypersensitive after her orgasm, his entry was nearly painful, but there was a raw, edgy bite to it that stirred her response and had her arching into him, wanting, needing more.

"And you, Callie? Has there been anyone else? Tell me, do I need to worry about protecting myself?"

Her eyes widened in shock and then she frowned but remained silent.

His nostrils flared, and he planted his palms on either side of her head and rocked his hips against her.

"Answer me. Has there been anyone else?"

He set a ruthless pace, driving her so close to the edge that she twisted and begged him to let her come. But he'd stop, just at the edge, and he'd watch her with cool green eyes as she went nearly frantic, trying to get him to move again.

"Max, please!"

"Tell me what I want to know, damn it. Tell me, and I'll let you come."

"No," she said brokenly. "There's never been anyone after you. I couldn't."

He lowered his head and kissed her softly on the mouth. He swallowed her soft sob and then slowed his thrusts. He began making love to her, so gentle and sweet.

Slowly and tenderly, he slid into her until the bite was replaced by waves of warm pleasure, seeping into her body and spreading like sunshine.

"Come, *dolcezza*," he whispered, and this time her release wasn't a violent explosion but rather an exquisite flow of honey, sweet through her veins.

Tears slipped down her cheeks as she tried valiantly to regain her composure. But he kissed each one away, sipping at the salt and then kissing her until she tasted the slight salt.

"I missed you so much," she said brokenly.

"And I missed you. So very much. You're mine, Callie. Mine. I'm not letting you go again."

Chapter Ten

Callie lay in Max's arms as the first rays of dawn crept through the window. He stroked her idly, his hand moving over the curves of her body to her hair. He bent and kissed her shoulder, sending a shiver of awareness over her aching body.

He'd made love to her the entire night. Raw and insatiable. He'd taken her to the very edge of her limits, and now she lay sated and exhausted but aware that for the first time in months she felt at peace.

He couldn't seem to get enough of her. Even now, his touch was possessive, like he was laying claim all over again.

"Tired?" he murmured, breaking the silence.

She nodded against him as the warm fuzz of sleep settled over her.

"Then sleep."

It wasn't as simple as that. She was almost afraid to close her eyes, worried that this was all a dream. A figment of her most earnest wishes. How many nights had she lain awake, wanting him so badly that it was a physical ache?

She turned, curling into his warm body. She tucked her head underneath his chin and let out a sigh of contentment.

"Do you know how many nights I've lain awake remembering how you felt in my arms?" he asked. "Or how you used to sigh like a contented kitten after we made love?"

She smiled against his chest.

"If you won't sleep, let's go out for an early breakfast. You can show me your town."

"I'd like that," she said softly.

He threaded his fingers into her hair and gently pulled through the strands. "I love your hair. I've never been able to figure out what color it is. It's a fascinating mix of black and chestnut with all these warm shades of brown mixed in. It reminds me of a sunset over the Greek isles."

She kissed his chest and slid her hand between them to let her fingers glide through the hair in the hollow of his chest.

"You were my best vacation ever," she joked lightly. "I've been so many places. But the trip where I met you was…magic."

"I'm amazed your family lets you crawl all over the world like you do. If you were mine, I'd worry endlessly about what you were getting into. I'd want to be with you to share in the joy of discovery."

She grimaced. "They worry. They've always worried. I don't think they understand me. They love me. They support me, but I don't think they've really ever understood what makes me tick or why I'm such a restless spirit."

He stroked up and down her arm and rested his cheek against hers. "What does make you so restless, Callie?"

She went silent a moment. "I love chasing sunsets. They look different everywhere I go. There's always something new to experience. My family is so…settled. Maybe I never felt like I really fit in."

She could feel him frown against her cheek.

"How so?"

She sighed. "My family is different. I told you I have three fathers. What you don't know is that after I came home, my three brothers fell in love with the same woman. It sounds so odd when I say it out loud, but it works for them. It works for my mom and my dads. Maybe in the back of my mind I figured, three sons ahead of me. It's sort of like a family tradition," she joked. "And then I come along, the only daughter in the mix. The only daughter in generations that I know of. Where was I going to fit in? Hell, everyone probably thinks I'm going to shack up with a few men too."

"Over my dead body," Max bit out.

She laughed. "Don't worry. I've never really understood the appeal. I love my fathers and my brothers dearly, but I wouldn't want to put up with that much testosterone in a relationship."

"I find I'm very possessive where you're concerned," he murmured.

She snorted. "You're possessive of everything you consider yours."

He seemed to consider that for a moment before he agreed. He nuzzled at her ear and then whispered, "Come on. Let's shower and then we'll go eat."

Half an hour later, they stepped into the crisp morning mountain air and a shiver shot up Callie's spine. Max frowned and then stripped off his jacket and settled it over her shoulders.

"You should have worn a coat."

She smiled up at him as he put an arm around her shoulders and drew her into his side. "I wasn't thinking much beyond getting to you. Besides, it'll warm up in a couple of hours and there'll be no need for a jacket."

He kissed her forehead and then they crossed the street to the busy café that had been a fixture of Clyde for longer than Callie had been alive.

As soon as they stepped inside, Callie could feel the gazes boring holes through her and Max. By noon, it would be all over town, and her mama would be the recipient of no less than a dozen calls all wondering who Callie's man was.

It didn't help that Max couldn't keep his hands off her. He had her snugly tucked against his body and his palm was splayed out over her hip. Anyone with eyes could see that Max had all but pissed on her and marked her.

The bell tinkled over the door as another customer came in.

"Crap," Callie murmured when she realized who it was.

"What's wrong?" Max asked.

"My brother."

"Which one?"

"Seth. The sheriff."

Max made no move to let her go as Seth approached. Callie recognized the look on Seth's face as the badass, intimidating freeze-out look he gave people he arrested. Not that he arrested many people in Clyde.

"Callie," Seth said in acknowledgement.

"Morning, Seth," she said cheerfully. "Where's Lily?"

"At home."

"Then what are you doing here?" Callie asked pointedly.

"I was at the office to pick up some paperwork when I saw you cross the street."

The accusing note in his voice told her very plainly he saw where she came from. At this hour of the morning and the fact she'd come from Max's hotel room, it was obvious where she'd spent the night.

"Going to introduce me, Callie?" Max smoothly interrupted.

Callie flashed a smile in Max's direction. "Max, this is my brother, Seth. Seth, this is Max Wilder."

Seth extended his hand but his expression was anything but welcoming. Callie wanted to kick him in the shin and would have if everyone in the café weren't glued to the unfolding scene.

"Would you care to join us?" Max asked as he shook Seth's hand.

Callie shot Seth a glare.

"No, maybe another time. Lily's expecting me home. She's cooking breakfast. Of course you could both join us for breakfast there," Seth said pointedly.

"Ah no, thanks though," Callie said quickly. "We already have plans."

Seth swept his gaze over Max once more, his stare sending a clear warning. It was that whole male thing that said *I'm watching you. Don't fuck up.* Callie rolled her eyes and tugged Max closer to the counter so they could order.

"Give Lily my love," Callie said and then stared pointedly at the door.

Seth shot her a disgruntled look. "Nice meeting you, Wilder." Though his tone suggested it was anything but.

He turned and walked back out the front door. Max and Callie waited in silence until it was their turn to order and then they took a seat in one of the booths facing the street.

Callie picked at her food and glanced periodically up at Max to gauge his reaction to Seth's obvious hostility.

"I have an apartment in Denver," Max said after he took a long drink of his coffee. "As much as I want to meet your family and allay their fears, I think it would be best if you and I spent some time alone so that when we do meet your family, you're happy again and you don't have those wounded shadows in your eyes."

Callie almost raised a hand to her eyes and she dropped her gaze guiltily.

"Callie, look at me."

She glanced back up to see Max staring intently at her.

"I hurt you. Your family knows I hurt you. I need to make you happy again before I meet them or they'll never believe in our relationship. You're still uncertain. I want you to be sure before we face them."

She slowly nodded her agreement.

"I'd like to take you to Denver for a week. There won't be any distractions there. Just you and me and whatever we want to do."

"I'd like that."

"Good. Then we'll leave after breakfast."

She blinked in surprise. "But I'll need to tell my mom. My dads. And I need to pack. All my things are at my parents'."

He reached over and slid his fingers over her hand. "All you need is you. I'll take care of the rest. You can call your parents on the way to Denver. I'll buy whatever it is you need."

Callie sighed. How Max did love to spoil her. And if she were completely honest, she'd admit she loved being pampered by him. He thought of everything and a few things she wouldn't.

He'd seen to her every need while they were in Europe. Her only task was pleasing him. Everything else, he took care of.

"All right," she agreed. "I'll call them on the way and let them know I'll be gone a week. They're used to me taking off on a whim, so it won't surprise them."

He raised her hand to his lips and pressed a soft kiss to her palm. "For the next week I'm going to love you, Callie. When we return, there won't be any doubt in your mind that I'd ever leave you again."

Chapter Eleven

Max glanced at Callie curled up in the seat next to him as he drove through downtown Denver. She was fast asleep, her knuckles tucked to her cheekbone, and her hair fanned out like a veil of silk.

She looked fragile and vulnerable in sleep. Underneath her eyes, shadows bruised the soft skin. He would take care of her this week. She'd sleep and rest, and she'd regain the sparkle in her eyes and the wide smile that lit up his world.

He'd spend every moment pampering her and loving her until she forgot what it was like to be without him. Until he could forget the long months he'd spent without her.

He pulled under the awning of the upscale high-rise apartment building and his door was quickly opened by the valet. Max held up a finger so that Callie wasn't awakened and the valet stepped back for Max to get out.

He walked around to the passenger side, opened Callie's door and then crouched beside her. He rubbed his fingers over her cheek and she stirred sleepily.

"Wake up, *dolcezza*. We're here."

Her eyelids fluttered open and his gaze was met by cloudy blue eyes. Then she looked beyond him and the fog fell away. She fumbled with her seat belt, but he stayed her hands and unbuckled her himself.

He helped her out of the car, gestured for the valet to take the wheel, and then he tucked her against him so she wouldn't get cold and walked past the doorman and into the building.

She was quiet as they got into the elevator. She stifled a yawn and then leaned into him after he inserted his card for the top floor. The action was so natural, as if they hadn't ever parted. She'd always been openly affectionate with him. So spontaneous. At first he hadn't known how to react. He was unused to such exuberance, but he'd quickly grown addicted to her displays of affection, and he lived for the times she snuggled into his arms or simply leaned into his touch as she was doing now.

He gathered her tight against him and kissed her brow as the elevator rose to the top floor. "Still tired?"

"Mmm-hmm," she murmured.

"Then we'll go to bed and you'll sleep some more."

She smiled. "So bossy. I'm fine. If I sleep more, I'll never go to bed tonight."

The elevator door opened into the foyer of his apartment and he urged Callie forward. Her eyes were wide as their feet tapped on the Italian marble.

"It's gorgeous, Max. So huge!"

It amused him how easily impressed she was. He knew her family was wealthy and yet somehow Callie was completely unaffected by it. It irritated him that with as much money as he knew her parents to have, she still backpacked over Europe, lived and ate like a poor student, and the vehicle she drove was ancient.

"I thought we'd take it easy today, and then tomorrow we'll go shopping for everything you need."

She wiped her hands down her jeans and then turned them

palms up. "This is it, Max. You wouldn't let me pack a bag. I don't have anything else to wear."

He smiled. "While you're here, I'd prefer you wear nothing. I'll make a call and have something delivered this evening for you to wear shopping tomorrow."

"Nothing?" She arched a brow and glanced at him as if gauging whether or not he was serious.

"Nothing at all," he murmured. "In fact, I'd like it a lot if you undressed now."

Her nose wrinkled. "I need a shower. Traveling makes me feel grimy."

"I'll draw you a bath or you can use the shower. Your choice."

"Or you could shower with me," she suggested impishly.

"Or I could take a shower with you," he agreed. "Afterward, we'll sit in front of the fire and I'll comb your hair for you."

"Oh, you do spoil me, Max," she said with a sigh. "No one has ever taken care of me like you."

He pulled her into his arms and kissed her nose. "That's a good thing. I'd prefer I do all the taking care of you."

Just the image of her in the shower all slicked down with water had him so hard he hurt. What he really wanted to do was to fuck her against the shower wall and then push her to her knees and have her suck him off while water beat down on them.

Only the fact that she looked tired and she hadn't slept the night before—not to mention he'd made love to her tirelessly and she was likely sore—kept him from stripping her down right then and there and hauling her into the shower to have her.

A little TLC wouldn't be remiss. Even if it killed him.

She leaned into him and hugged him as she snuggled her face into his chest. He loved that. Loved how warm and soft she felt in his arms and how she melted against him.

He circled her body with his arms and squeezed, content to just hold her.

Finally he pulled away and laced his fingers through hers. He tugged her toward the master bedroom and the huge bathroom with the Jacuzzi tub and the separate shower.

He left her long enough to turn on the water and then he returned. When she would have begun undressing, he gently captured her wrist.

"Let me."

She lowered her hand and curled her fingers into a fist at her side. Her blue eyes darkened to storm clouds and hunger flared.

Sometimes it was painful to be around her. They never seemed to get enough. The passion between them was a living, breathing thing. He'd never experienced such a raw desperation for a woman and certainly hadn't had a woman respond to him as Callie did.

They were matching halves. Their chemistry was perfect. She was perfect.

Beautiful, submissive, so hungry to please and to be pleased.

He could be himself with her. He didn't have to pretend. He didn't have to hold back. She took everything he gave her and wanted—no demanded—more.

She wasn't offended by his need to control—to dominate. She offered herself so sweetly that it made his gut ache. No one had ever given themselves so freely. And he had tried his best to fuck it up.

All because of a promise.

He shook away the unwelcome intrusion of his darker thoughts and unsnapped Callie's jeans. Steam began rising from the shower and he eased the pants down her legs.

Leaving them bunched around her ankles, he pulled at her shirt until she was clad in just her bra and panties.

Unable to resist, he knelt in front of her and pressed a kiss to the silky V of her underwear. Her mound was soft beneath and teased his lips. Frustrated with the barrier, he thumbed the band and worked the lace over her hips until the soft triangle of hair was exposed to his gaze.

"You're so soft and feminine."

He rose up and tongued her navel and then nibbled a path around it. She thrust her fingers into his hair and held his head against her body as he kissed her lovingly.

"Step away," he directed as he rose to his feet.

She kicked out of her jeans and underwear, and then he pulled her against his chest until her breasts pushed over the cups of her bra.

"Perfect. Just perfect."

He cupped one and lifted until her nipple peeked over the peach-colored lace of her bra. The delicate coral peak beckoned him, and he lowered his head. He flicked out his tongue and traced the top of her areola until her nipple puckered and poked rigidly outward.

Another little push and her breast was free from the cup. He rubbed his tongue over the bud and then sucked it between his teeth.

She gasped and stumbled. He wrapped an arm around her waist and held her tightly as he licked and teased the delicious treat.

"Shower's ready."

"Tease," she grumbled.

He grinned and all but carried her backward through the open shower door and into the hot spray. She immediately let out a groan of pleasure as the heat sluiced over them both.

He prodded until her head fell back, baring her neck to his seeking mouth. Despite his determination not to start anything, he found he couldn't stop himself. She was an addiction. A fire in his blood he hadn't a hope of quenching.

Breathing hard, he tore himself from the taste of her skin and stood back for a moment to collect himself.

She reached for the shampoo, but he wrested it from her grip and dumped some of the liquid into his hand. He began at the top of her head and worked the shampoo into her hair. After he rinsed, he grabbed a washcloth and tormented them both by soaping every inch of her delectable body from head to toe, paying extra attention to the parts in between.

When he was done, she took the cloth, squeezed soap into it and then started at his chest. By the time she reached his belly, he was hard as a rock and so swollen it felt like he was going to split at the seams.

Her sweet hands worked around his cock and down to his balls, where she cupped and rolled, driving him more insane by the minute.

When she stepped away to rinse the soap, he groaned. She sent him a pouty, sultry look that only made him want to press her against the wall of the shower and fuck her senseless.

As water rained down over her, she came back to him and lowered to her knees in front of him. He guessed her intention and reached down to grasp his cock and pull it away from her grasp.

"No, baby. You don't have to. You're tired."

She gently tugged his hand away from his cock and curled her fingers around the base. "I want to," she said in a husky voice.

His breath hissed explosively from his throat as she slowly slid her tongue over his length. The warm water had nothing on the heat of her mouth. She sucked him deep, licked over his rigid flesh and then slowly pulled away until the tip of his cock hung precariously from her lips.

She lapped at the slit and made a purring sound deep in her throat, thready with contentment.

"Jesus, Callie."

"Help me," she murmured. "Show me how you like it, Max."

"You know damn well how I like it," he growled.

But even as he spoke, his hands were on the sides of her face, gripping and holding her in place as he guided his cock inside and then deep. He held himself there for a long moment and then withdrew, sliding across her tongue.

She was the most erotic sight he'd ever witnessed in his life. On her knees, slicked down, water running in rivulcts ovcr her breasts, her face turned up and her gaze fastened on him. Awaiting his command.

He stroked her cheekbones with his thumbs and spread his fingers gently over her ears to the slick hair behind them. Her mouth was the sweetest fire he'd ever immersed himself in.

Hot. Tight. Wet.

So damn good he was going to lose his mind, his control, his very soul.

She surrounded him like liquid velvet. Sweet. Fiery beyond his wildest imaginings.

Each stroke to the back of her throat brought him that

much closer to absolute abandon. She swallowed around his cock, her throat working around his flesh with wicked skill that left him shuddering uncontrollably.

"Let me taste you, Max. I want everything."

Her soft plea unhinged him. He stroked deep as his release coiled tight in his balls and surged up his cock. The head of his penis rubbed over the top of her mouth and to the soft tissues at the back of her throat. She swallowed the first spurt of his semen, and the motion shattered the last of his control.

He gripped her head and thrust. Hard. His orgasm was painful. Ripped from him like he was shedding his skin. Intense bursts of ecstasy splintered through his groin and his knees nearly buckled as he exploded in her mouth.

He threw back his head, slammed his eyes shut and clenched his teeth so tightly that pain shot through his jaw.

She continued to stroke and caress him, coaxing the last of his release from his still-hard dick. Each little pet sent another shudder rocketing through his body. Little electric impulses that had him groaning as wave after wave of endless pleasure silvered through his veins.

He slipped from her mouth, but she continued to glide her fingers over his hypersensitive flesh, her hands working their delicious magic.

Suddenly aware of the water still streaming down over Callie, he reached quickly to turn off the shower. He felt like a drunk trying to stagger out of a bar as he took a step through the shower door.

His legs were rubbery and aftershocks still sparked through his body, but his first duty was to Callie.

He grabbed a towel off the rack and reached back for Callie's hand to help her out of the shower. When she stood, dripping on the floor, he engulfed her in the towel and gently rubbed her from head to toe.

She sighed a little wistfully as he moved to her hair and began wiping the moisture from the long strands.

"I should be drying you," she murmured.

He leaned in to kiss the corner of her mouth. "Huh-uh, *dolcezza*. You know how much I love taking care of you. And you already took such good care of me in the shower. For the next little while, I'm going to pamper and spoil you ridiculously."

She smiled. "I like ridiculously. You do ridiculously really well."

"I should hope so."

He wrapped her hair in a towel, and then he retrieved the plush robe from the hook on the back of the door and pulled it around her body until she was engulfed by the thick terrycloth.

"Go in the living room and wait for me," he directed. "It'll just take me a minute to get dressed."

Chapter Twelve

Callie walked into the living room, drawing the robe tighter around her. It wasn't that it was cold. In fact, the apartment was at a perfect temperature. Heat rose from the floors and a fire blazed in the hearth though she guessed it was a gas log.

Still, it looked inviting and she went to stand in front of it. When she turned her back to warm the hands she held behind her, she stared out the opposing window to the view of downtown Denver and distant mountains.

In a lot of ways, this reminded her of traveling across Greece and Italy with Max. She'd always backpacked and stayed in hostels or slept in train stations. Max was horrified at the idea that a young woman for all practical purposes was operating as a homeless person.

Callie had laughed and said for all practical purposes he was right. She had money but it had to be strictly rationed, and if she could get cheap accommodations or a place to camp, then she didn't have to dip into her cash reserve, which meant she could travel even longer.

Max had put an end to all that from the moment Callie first let him make love to her. He'd taken over—not in an overbearing, assholish way—but rather he wanted to take care of her and proceeded to do just that.

He was firm. He was stubborn. But he wasn't a jerk who

got off on giving her orders.

She smiled as she remembered one particular conversation they'd shared in one of the sumptuous hotel rooms he'd reserved. She was on her knees on a thick, plush carpet not unlike the one in his apartment now.

Max had rubbed his hand up and down her cheek in an affectionate caress and asked, "Do I have your obedience, Callie?"

She wrinkled her nose and curled her lip in distaste. "I don't like that word. I'm not a child. You aren't my parents. I'm not some wayward twit who needs to be kept in line. Surely there has to be a better way to get your point across, Max. You know I love pleasing you. I *need* to please you. But please don't use words like obedience, because it suggests something I don't like."

He smiled and leaned down to kiss her furrowed brow. "You worry too much, *dolcezza.* I never want to make you uncomfortable, to degrade you or make you feel any less than you are. If I ever cross that line, I hope you will, in true Callie fashion, kick my ever-loving ass."

She grinned back at him. "You bet your ass."

His face grew serious once more and he touched her cheek again. "Do I have your submission?"

She thought for a long moment about what he was asking for. To some, obedience and submission were probably the same thing. Not to her. Obedience suggested blind loyalty. No free will. Submission suggested a choice. A choice to place herself in the care of another. But with conditions. Trust. Always trust. Obedience didn't necessarily equate to trust.

If someone was in a position of authority over another, they could command obedience and it would be far different than Callie offering her submission to Max. To give her care and trust to this man.

Finally she looked up at him, her brows drawn in seriousness. "Yes, Max. You have my submission. Willingly and joyfully."

Callie sighed at the remembrance, and a shiver of delight skittered over her shoulders. They'd spent so many wonderful nights together. She'd submitted without regret. Until the day he'd left and hadn't returned.

Frowning at the unhappy turn of her thoughts, she hugged her arms and walked away from the fire. She unwound the towel from her hair and dropped it on the floor as she came to stand in front of the window.

She didn't hear Max's approach. Didn't know he was behind her until his hands closed over her shoulders and he brushed a kiss over her temple.

She turned instinctively into the warmth and comfort of his body. He hugged her close, wrapping those strong arms around her, and she tucked her head underneath his chin.

"I wonder if you know how glad I am to have you back where you belong."

She smiled but didn't say anything for a moment. It was easy to pretend that they'd never separated and that this was just an extension of the time they'd spent together in Europe.

Maybe he sensed her hesitancy because he pulled away and stared down at her with his intense gaze.

"What are you thinking?"

She started to respond but then wondered if she should really voice what she'd been thinking. She didn't want to ruin what had been a perfect afternoon.

Max frowned and then tugged her toward the couch. He settled on the end and then pulled her down onto his lap until she was curled in his arms, her back against the arm of the sofa.

"Don't pull any punches, Callie. Not with me. Whatever it is you were about to say, just say it. We won't be able to move forward until we clear the air."

She sighed and leaned her head over until it was pillowed on his shoulder. "I was just thinking about Europe. It was such a fantasy, so dreamlike when we were together. Every day was so perfect and I wondered if it was too good to be true. Then when you left and I finally came home, I convinced myself that's all it was. Just a fantasy. It wasn't meant to last."

She shifted so she could look at him. She felt she owed it to him for what she was about to say.

"I wondered if that's what this is. Another fantasy. Something too good to be true and if it will disappear just like before. I wonder if I'm deluding myself, and worse, I wonder how stupid I am for allowing it to happen all over again when I know you have so much power to hurt me."

She thought he might be angry, but she couldn't be anything less than honest. His answer surprised her, though.

"I understand why you feel that way," he said roughly. "I don't blame you. I know I'm asking a lot, particularly because I'm not only asking you for another chance, but I'm asking for your complete and utter trust. I'm asking you to cede power to me. I'm asking for your submission—again."

She swallowed and nodded, glad that at least he understood her conflict. And her fear.

He smoothed his fingers over her still-damp hair, his gaze so intent on her that she had no doubt of his sincerity.

"I want you, Callie. I want us. I want to see where this takes us. I've tried it without you. I was miserable, and I think you were too. I think we're better together."

"I want us too," she whispered. "There's so much to talk about, though. So much we didn't cover in Europe. I don't even know what you do. My family asked, and I felt like the worst sort of idiot. I know *nothing* about you. And yet you know so much about me."

Max pressed his lips to her forehead in a gesture so tender that her chest tightened. "That is what this week is for, *dolcezza*. Us. So that when we go meet your family, there is no doubt to anyone looking at us that you're happy and confident."

Her heart fluttered at the endearment he'd teasingly begun when they were in Italy. He'd taught her words of love and affection in many languages, but *dolcezza* had been her favorite. His eyes always burned a little brighter when he called her that.

"And to begin our week, I want you naked. I love the feel of your skin. I love the beauty of your body. My desire is that when we are in private I am never deprived of your sweetness."

He pulled gently at the tie and then helped her to her feet. He stood in front of her and carefully peeled away the robe until she was naked in front of him, her skin soft and warm from the shower.

"*Bellissima*," he murmured. "You are very beautiful, *dolcezza*. Even more so because you're mine."

He reached for a comb lying on the end table and then sat back on the couch, spreading his thighs. He patted the space between his legs.

"Sit so I can comb your hair while it's still damp."

She turned and then settled on the edge of the couch. His hands slipped over her hips as he steadied her, and then they wandered up her waist and around to cup her breasts.

He toyed idly with her nipples until they were rigid, and then he slid his hands up over her shoulders and gathered her hair at her nape.

"I love having the freedom to touch you however and whenever I want."

"You're such a spoiled man," she teased.

"When it comes to you, I am."

"You're such a caveman."

"And this is a problem?" he asked as he began working the comb through the ends of her hair.

"Evidently not." She sighed. "I can't resist you even when your knuckles are dragging the ground and you grunt stuff like 'my woman'."

"Damn right you're my woman. What else am I supposed to say?"

She chuckled. "If I have to tell you then you require more work than I'm willing to put in to make you civilized."

"Admit it, you love that I'm completely uncivilized."

"Yes, I do, and I don't want to know what that says about me."

"It says you're a woman with intelligent, discerning tastes."

"You're incorrigible!"

"You love me."

She bit her lip when she would have said indeed she did. He'd said it in a light, teasing way. Like someone would say to a friend. *Oh, you love me.*

Only she did love him. So much it hurt. But it was the one part of herself she did hold back from him. Despite the fact that she'd forgiven him. She was willing to try again. She'd give him another chance. But she'd be a fool to make herself utterly vulnerable to him. Not yet.

"Tell me about you," she said quietly. "What makes you

who you are, Max?"

"That's a loaded question."

She shrugged. "Maybe. But it shouldn't be a difficult question. It shouldn't cause you any issue to answer."

She could picture his brows knitting as he pondered the best way to answer. He paused for a moment, his fingers tangled in her hair, the comb still in his hand. Then he began combing again. Long, steady strokes. Infinitely gentle.

"I made my fortune at a young age. For me it was necessity, not so much desire. It wasn't that I craved fine things. Or even money. For me money wasn't about the luxuries it could provide, but the necessities and what I could give to my mother and my sister.

"I wanted my mother not to have to worry. I wanted her to have the same lifestyle she had when she was married to my stepfather. I wanted my sister to go to the best schools and have all she needed."

"How did you do all that? You make it sound so simple."

He tugged at one particularly difficult tangle and then carefully worked out the snarl.

"I worked my ass off. Two, sometimes three jobs. Every penny I made at first was saved to buy my first property. I sold it for a ten-thousand-dollar profit and you'd have thought I hung the moon. I used all of it to make my next investment and with the second sale, I made a whopping six-figure profit. Part of it was luck. Being in the right place at the right time, but just as much of it was determination to succeed. Failure simply wasn't an option."

That she could believe. She couldn't imagine Max failing at anything he set his mind to. To hear his story only confirmed what she already knew. Max was driven. He was ruthless when he had to be.

She shivered with sudden realization. He'd made it clear that she was his current ambition. And if his past was anything to go by, she didn't have a chance in hell of resisting him.

But then she didn't really want to.

Was she a temporary challenge? Had he pursued other women as he'd done her?

Silence fell between them as he continued his careful combing of her hair. He was meticulous, separating each of the strands and working the tangles out.

She wondered how much experience he had with taking care of other women. The thought was unwelcome and painful. It was also stupid. His past was just that. His past. Just like he couldn't hold any of her past lovers against her. But it still cut at her to think of other women under his care. Submitting to him as she was submitting to him.

She frowned again. Had he had such relationships in the past? Surely he had. He was simply too comfortable and too adept at seeing to her every need. He was arrogant but not in a petulant fashion. He wore arrogance like it was his due. Like he was convinced, not trying to convince others.

And he was extremely confident and comfortable as someone always in control.

"You're tense. What are you thinking now?"

She blushed. Heat crawled over her skin as he caught her out again.

"Callie," he prompted.

"It's just that you're very good at this," she mumbled. "I wondered how many other women you've shared this sort of *relationship* with."

"Do you really want to know?" he asked bluntly. "Or are you just torturing yourself?"

She winced. "Both, I guess. It's natural to be curious. And natural to discuss prior relationships. Don't you think? Isn't this the sort of thing all couples get into after a while?"

"I suppose it is. It's a sticky subject though. If you aren't prepared for the answer or if it hurts you, it's best not to ask."

"Yeah, yeah, I know. Never ask for an answer you aren't prepared to receive."

"I propose that I finish combing your hair, and then I need to make a few business calls. I've already made arrangements for dinner to be delivered as well as something for you to wear tomorrow. Those things should be arriving soon. Then, if you still want to have this discussion, we'll talk about it while we eat."

She nodded her agreement.

"Relax," he murmured. "You're supposed to be enjoying this."

She closed her eyes, leaned back and once more allowed the pleasure of his attentions to seep back into her veins. But still, the image of another woman in her place unsettled her.

Chapter Thirteen

Callie sat on the couch with her feet curled beneath her as she listened to Max make his phone calls. Earlier he'd ordered clothing for her. He hadn't asked her sizes. Not even for her girly things, and somehow she knew he'd gotten them right. Which further confirmed her suspicion that he'd been around the block more than a few times.

And it didn't bother her. Not really. Not in the sense that she was about to become an insanely jealous, crazy girlfriend. But she wondered. Not over his relationships exactly. But Max was a man who liked things his way. He became entrenched. He liked routine. He didn't like change.

So what had happened to those other women? Had he discarded them as he'd done her? Okay so technically he hadn't discarded her since he'd come looking for her. But had he grown bored with his other relationships? Would he become bored with her?

She hated all the doubts, but the one thing she'd come to realize in the months after she'd returned home was that for as much time as she'd spent with Max, for as much of herself as she'd given him, they hadn't ever discussed the future. Their relationship had been very much in the now. Live for the moment.

No past. No future. Only the present.

She glanced over to where he stood murmuring in low tones on the phone. He'd only just offered her a glimpse into his past. He now spoke of the future. That should reassure her. Shouldn't it?

Her gaze left him, and her lips pursed as she contemplated the complexity of her relationship with Max. In so many ways, he was an enigma, though finally she was beginning to scratch the surface. This time around she wasn't going to be content with just what he offered her peripherally. She wanted the whole package. She'd been so blinded by her infatuation and then love for him, that she made the mistake so many people made when a relationship was all shiny and new. She hadn't taken the time to get to know him on a much deeper level.

"Are you cold?"

Callie looked up and realized that while she'd been lost in her thoughts, Max had finished his calls and was now standing in front of her.

She glanced down her nude body and then shook her head.

"Good. If you're going to be naked, and I prefer you that way, I want to make sure the apartment is kept at a comfortable temperature for you."

"What about..."

He raised an eyebrow and waited.

"What about when people come in? I mean like when dinner is delivered."

He crouched down in front of her and slid his hand down the curve of her hip to her knee and then up again. "No one else will see you, Callie. I'm fiercely protective of what's mine. No one will be allowed inside the apartment while you are here unless you're appropriately attired."

"And do I eat nekkid?" she asked with a grin.

"Oh yes," he murmured. "I can't imagine a better meal than to have you nude in front of me. You'll eat from my hand. I'll see to your every need."

She shivered at the husky thrall of his voice. She'd been completely his in Europe but now she realized she'd only gotten a taste of his dominance. They'd still been on the cusp of something new, still finding their way, and he'd likely held some of himself in reserve until she was more comfortable with him.

"Tell me something, Max. Is my submission contained only to the bedroom or do you expect me to cede control to you in all aspects of my life?"

He rubbed his thumb over her nipple, teasing it to a rigid peak. "You're asking a lot of questions, and I'm unsure whether you're prepared for the answers."

"I want your honesty," she said. "I'm not some fragile little flower who wilts because your answers aren't all pretty and sweet. You told me not to ask if I wasn't prepared for the answer. I have a lot I want to ask."

"Fair enough."

A buzz sounded and Max got to his feet. He rubbed his hand underneath her chin and slid his thumb across her cheek. "Hold that thought while I collect dinner and the things I ordered for you. We'll discuss whatever you like while we eat."

Callie waited as he went to answer the buzzer. She heard him say in low tones that he'd go down to get it. She smiled. He really didn't want to risk her being seen by anyone but him.

A few moments later, he walked back into the living room carrying several boxes. He dumped them next to the couch and then left once more only to return with a rolling cart bearing several covered plates.

He parked it in front of the couch and set to work taking the covers off and preparing plates of the steaming pasta. The aroma tantalized her and her stomach growled in response. There was fresh bread—her weakness. Fresh parmesan and a bottle of chilled wine in an ice bucket.

Max settled on the couch next to her but placed the plate on the coffee table.

"I want you on your knees in front of the couch. So I can feed you better."

Her eyes widened, and for a moment she hesitated as she tried to picture what he'd asked her to do.

"Callie?"

Slowly she sat forward and then slid to her knees on the floor at his feet. She turned as he too sat forward, his thigh brushing the side of her face.

"Perfect," he said, approval purring in his voice.

He held a glass of wine to her mouth and carefully tilted it so she could take a sip. Then he pulled it away and forked a small bite of the pasta. Raising it to his mouth, he gently blew and touched it to his lips before lowering it and offering it to her.

There was something amazingly seductive about the way he made sure the food was perfect for her. He was careful to keep the bites the right size and he never offered it to her without testing it himself.

His gaze held hers, smoky and seductive, never leaving her face as he placed another bite to her lips. He waited as she savored the decadent morsel and then offered another sip of wine.

He was remarkably patient, never tiring as he held the fork to her mouth. At one point she smeared a bit of the sauce on the corner of her mouth and when she would have licked it away, he put his hand out to stop her and then lowered his mouth to swipe at the spot with his tongue.

Warm and rough, his tongue slid across her mouth, pausing at the corner where he lightly lapped and sucked until the sauce was gone. A shiver skirted down her spine. Her body leapt to attention and her pulse sped up, jumping at her pulse points.

When he pulled away, his breath huffed jerkily and his nostrils flared. His eyes glittered with awareness, and his hand shook just a bit as he pulled it away to fork another piece of the pasta.

He raised the wineglass and pressed his lips to the same place where her mouth had been. He took a long swallow before lowering it to the coffee table.

"More?"

She shook her head wordlessly.

He didn't take a single bite until she was sated. She'd been so mesmerized by the experience that they hadn't spoken. She hadn't asked any questions, nor had he offered explanations.

Only when she assured him with a nod that she'd had enough did he refill his plate and begin to eat. After taking only one bite, he put his fork down and slid his hand through her hair. Then he gently tugged until her cheek lay on top of his lap and her head was cradled against him.

He rubbed her cheek, a silent directive for her to remain as he'd positioned her and then he resumed his meal.

They didn't speak and yet the connection between them was powerful. Instead of being awkward, the silence was comforting. She felt close to him. Like they'd shared an intimacy much like making love.

There was a strange, achy tightness to her chest and yet there was also a sense of homecoming, like this was right after so long being wrong.

Finally she was back where she most needed to be. She closed her eyes as she rested against his thigh and sighed contentedly.

A moment later, his hand cupped her head and stroked over her hair. Then he reached down for her hand and helped her to her feet. She rose to stand before him, a little self-conscious as he stared at her nude body.

"Come sit with me," he said as he steered her toward the overstuffed chair across from the couch.

He sat first and then pulled her onto his lap until she was cuddled against his chest.

"Now ask these questions you want answered," he said. "We're full, I'm holding you. I'm a happy man."

She smiled ruefully as his fingers glided over her breast and he toyed with one nipple as he awaited her response. The man made it hard to want anything other than for him to hold her and to keep touching her.

"Have there been other women like me?"

He laughed softly. "Now there is an easy question to answer. No, there has never been another woman like you. I think it's safe to say that you're one of a kind, Callie."

She pulled away just enough that she could look into his eyes. "I meant women that you've had a dominant/submissive relationship with. When did you know that this is what you wanted, or have you always known? What happened to the other women?"

Max sighed. "I've had several relationships, not all of which have been as a dominant to the woman's submissive. The ones I've been the happiest in and the most content, however, were with a submissive woman. I've found those to be the most rewarding.

"As to what happened to those women, the relationship simply didn't work out."

"Why not?"

He looked vexed by her question. For a long moment he stared away and then finally he looked back at her. Something dark flashed in his eyes, something that sent a little shiver pricking up her nape.

"They weren't willing to go as far as I wanted them. But more than that, I think I recognized that I had selfish reasons for wanting their submission. It was all about me. How they could please me. It was no wonder I found no satisfaction in those relationships. And then you..."

"What about me? Why was I different? Why *am* I different?"

"Because it was no longer about me when I was with you," he said. "It wasn't a game, some idle pleasure. It wasn't something I wanted. It was something I *needed.* I needed you. I needed your submission. Not simply because it would please me. But because I wanted to take care of *you*, cherish you, protect you and love you. I wanted to please you more than I wanted to be pleased."

His answer lay heavy between them. Her heart thudded more forcefully against her chest. He sounded so...impassioned. Like every word had been wrenched from the very depths of his soul.

Max swallowed and blew out his breath. "We talked about why I left. Why I stayed gone. The fact that we fell so hard and heavy and fast. The truth is, from the moment I met you, Callie, my thoughts about you were dark and all-consuming. I pushed you hard and you took everything I gave you and wanted more. That scared the hell out of me. It seemed too..."

"Too what?"

"Perfect. Too damn perfect."

Her brows drew together in confusion.

"I looked at you and saw someone who was perfect for me in every way. Someone who met my needs. All of them. But there was so much more I wanted from you and I had to make a decision whether to trust that you were that perfect person for me or whether I wanted to back away before I became too emotionally involved with you."

It sounded cold. Clinical. Harsh even. She stared pensively at him for a long time, mulling over his words. Despite the bald way he put it out there, she sensed vulnerability.

"So you backing away was self-preservation."

He rubbed a hand over his face and then through his hair. "Yes. I suppose you could call it that. I needed time to evaluate. I needed to be sure that you would be happy in the relationship I would demand."

"You're an idiot, Max."

He blinked in surprise and his brows drew together as he glared at her.

"You men never get it right. Half the time you don't think at all and then the times you do think, you think too much."

"Care to explain my idiocy?"

"Did it never occur to you to talk to me? I don't know, maybe ask me if I was comfortable in our relationship? Maybe lay out what more you wanted from me and gauge my reaction?"

"I was worried we moved too fast, that we jumped without thinking and were caught up in the moment. I thought we needed distance so we could think with clear heads."

"Now you're calling *me* an idiot," she muttered.

He sighed. "I'm doing no such thing, Callie. And if it makes you feel any better, I knew I'd made a huge mistake. I was miserable without you, and the truth is, even if you weren't comfortable giving me all I demanded from you, I wanted you badly enough to compromise. I swore to myself I'd take whatever you were willing to give."

She touched his cheek, grazing the tips of her finger lightly over his jaw. "I would have given you *anything*, Max."

"Have I ruined it then? Will you punish us both by withholding what we both want?"

"I'm not vindictive. I try not to be. You hurt me. We both know that. I'm still dealing with that but I'm working on it. I want to be happy. I'm tired of feeling sad. I want to be happy with you."

"I'll make you happy, Callie."

She lifted her mouth to his and gave him a soft kiss. His hand glided up her leg, over the curve of her buttocks and up her waist until he cupped her breast.

"Tell me what you want," she whispered. "How much of my submission are you demanding?"

His eyes glittered as she pulled away. He stared back at her until she burned under his gaze. "Everything. I want everything. Nothing less."

Chapter Fourteen

Max never took his eyes off Callie as she digested his blunt declaration. She didn't flinch. Didn't shy away. Nor did she appear to have an extreme reaction.

Her expression didn't change but she cocked her head to the side and stared at him like she was sliding into his thoughts and giving them serious consideration.

"Define everything, Max. Are you being dramatic to make a point? I need you to be exacting here. This isn't the sort of thing we can afford to misunderstand."

He almost smiled. So typically Callie. Blunt. To the point. She wasn't a shy woman. He'd been afraid that he'd ruined some of that spirit, but it was there. Maybe beaten down, but it stirred beneath the shadows and slowly flickered to life.

"What do I mean by everything? It's simple and yet complicated. You asked before if you were to submit to me only in the bedroom, so in essence you were asking if it was narrowed to sex. My answer is no."

He thumbed over her nipple, unable to keep from touching her. He'd never grow tired of feeling her against him. After so many months, it was like coming home to have her in his arms. He could sit here all night and simply touch her and smell her.

"I want you to be mine. You'll be mine to protect. To cherish. To love. To take care of. To provide for. I want to dress you, spoil you, lavish you with fine food. Trips to Europe, the world. I want you to trust me enough to allow me to make the decisions in our relationship. To cede absolute control to me in the bedroom. To give your body to me and only me. But it's not about you giving and me taking. It's not about pleasing me to the exclusion of all else. Maybe it was like that in my other relationships. I want ours to be about me pleasing you every bit as much as you please me. I want to do things for you. Everything for you. I want to give you things. I want this kind of relationship for what it can do for you as well as me. For the things I can give to you.

"So, no, I don't want it confined to the bedroom, but I want our relationship to be where you can push back when I go too far. But only then. Once we establish complete trust, it will be easier. You'll know that I won't *want* to do anything that isn't in your best interests."

Her brows bunched and she stared intently at him. Her expression was pensive, and he knew she'd absorbed every single one of his words and even now was turning them over and over in her mind. He could see the questions in her eyes.

He smiled. She wanted to argue. To protest. But she tempered the bubbling protest as she continued to study him.

"It takes a very strong woman to submit to a man," he said as he fingered a strand of her hair. "What attracted me to you was your beauty and your laughter. I'll never forget the first time I saw you in Italy. You took my breath away. But later, it was your fiercely independent spirit that kept me with you. Even as you submitted, your will remained. Your true self was unaltered. You retained all the qualities I most admired, and yet you offered your submission to me so sweetly it made me ache."

"You seem so sure the two can coexist long-term," she said. "Is that what happened with your other women? Did they lose themselves in the process?"

Her intuitive question caught him off guard. "Partly, yes. It happened in two of my relationships. They were so caught up in pleasing me that they became shells of the women I was first attracted to. They became...what they thought I wanted. What I thought I wanted for that matter. It sounds so contradictory, but what I want is a woman who can please me and be pleased by me, but not lose herself in the process. Someone strong. Someone like you."

"I may have misjudged you, Max," she offered quietly. "All this while I've been hurting and aching, and I assumed you weren't thinking about me at all, that you left me without thought and never looked back. But that's not true, is it? You've been thinking about me—us—quite a lot."

"Not a day has passed that I haven't thought about us."

Her eyes softened and became damp pools of blue. She reached up and cupped his cheek and stroked gently. "You have my submission, Max. Without reservation. I want to try. I don't know if you're right and I'm the woman you need or that I'll end up being the woman you want, but I want to be her. I'm willing to try. I'm willing to give us a chance. I'll make mistakes. I've never allowed anyone the kind of control you're asking for."

He smiled and leaned forward to kiss her on the forehead. "I've no doubt no one has ever been able to control you. And that's not what I want to do. I love your free spirit too much. I am the only person I ever want you to submit to and it's my job to cherish your gift and not crush your spirit but nurture it instead."

She smiled back. "I think I can handle that."

"Good. Now that we've settled that matter, I want to establish a few ground rules."

She started to frown but recovered quickly and instead

looked inquisitively at him.

"When we are alone, whether in this apartment or elsewhere, you aren't to wear clothing unless I've said otherwise."

Her lips parted and he could see her battling over whether to question him.

"I want you accessible to me at all times. If I want to fuck you in the kitchen, I want to be able to just lean you over the table and slide inside your sweet body."

Her breathing hiccupped and her eyes went a little hazy.

"I might want you to suck my cock while I eat after I've fed you. I prefer for you to be nude when that occurs."

Her lips quivered and she twitched in his lap. He almost grinned. She was getting turned on by the images he painted.

"When we're in the living room, I want to be able to bend you over the arm of the couch and fuck you from behind. Or I might want to sit on the sofa and have you sit on my cock. The point is I want you accessible at all times. I want to be able to look at you whenever I want and touch you."

She nodded jerkily but kept silent.

"Tomorrow when we go shopping, I'm going to choose jewelry for you to wear. It will be a sign of my ownership. At no time will you take it off. You will only do so if we're no longer together."

Her eyes widened again. "You mean like a...collar?"

His heart softened at the horror in her voice. "No, *dolcezza.* A collar would never do for you. It would be demeaning. You would hate it. And me for making you do such a thing. What I have in mind are wrist cuffs. I want them specially designed for you and engraved with my name."

"Oh," she said with a quiet sigh. "I don't think that would

be bad at all."

He nudged her chin up with his fingers. "Callie, we need to make something clear. Yes, I expect your submission, however, this isn't a dictatorship. You have to tell me if at any time you're uncomfortable with something. The last thing I want is for you to be unhappy. We'll talk about it and work something out."

She smiled and it lit up her entire face.

"When we're in public, I don't expect you to assume the role of my submissive. The only thing you will be to others is the woman I adore and cherish above all others. Our private life is exactly that. Private. I don't need the world to see you submit. I'm the only person who ever needs to see it."

He circled her wrist with his fingers and her pulse sped up, racing against his hand.

"You're seducing me with mere words," she whispered. "You always do."

He picked up her hand and pressed his lips to her wrist and then her palm, and then he kissed each fingertip until he curled her hand and brushed his mouth across her knuckles.

"You'll sleep in my bed every night. The last thing you'll feel before you go to sleep is me inside you. The first thing you'll feel when you wake up is me inside you."

She jerked and shuddered against him, and her breaths came out in short little huffs like she couldn't quite keep up.

"I'll push your limits," he said in a serious tone. "There's a lot we haven't done that we'll do. Your body will be mine and that means that I'll do with you as I like. I'm not a masochist. I have no interest in taking things so far that you'll fear me or not enjoy what I do to you. But some of what I do will be for my pleasure and my pleasure alone just as there will be times when I'll want to give you pleasure while taking none in return."

"Is that all?" she asked as she licked her dry lips.

He kissed those lips and ran his tongue over top and bottom until they glistened.

"No. There is something I'd like to mention and get out in the open. You've told me about your fathers. And now your brothers. I don't pretend to understand the arrangement. You haven't said a lot other than they were in a committed polyamorous relationship. I'm not even sure what that means in the real world. So I'll just get this out. I'm not comfortable with sharing you. Ever." He snorted. "Comfortable is too soft a word to use here. You never hinted that you wanted a similar relationship to the one your mother and sister-in-law have, but it isn't happening. Over my dead body. I'll take apart any son of a bitch I ever find in your bed and then I'll kick your pretty ass all over the country."

Callie shook with silent laughter. It was obvious she tried really hard to keep it in. Then she cracked and started laughing out loud. He glared at her the whole time as she wiped tears from her cheeks.

"Oh God, Max," she gasped out. "You crack me up. That's the funniest thing I've ever heard."

"What's so damn funny? Your whole family is involved in some weird relationship where the women sleep with multiple men. I'm just trying to save us all some grief by telling you now it isn't going to happen, and if it does, someone's going to die."

She snickered again and wiped frantically at her eyes. Then she clutched his face in both hands and kissed him hot, hard and breathless.

"I have no desire to sleep with more than one man," she said. "I realize my parents' situation is...unusual."

Max lifted one eyebrow. "Unusual?"

She scowled. "Okay maybe it's strange but not to me or

them. It's what I grew up with. And the thing is my dads love my mom more than anything. That woman is pampered, spoiled and adored more than any woman I know other than my sister-in-law. And they all love me."

Max softened and pulled her closer to him until she was cuddled tight against his chest and her nipples poked through his chest hair. "I don't doubt they love you with all their heart and soul, *dolcezza.* How could they do anything else? I don't mean to demean them. I just can't wrap my head around the idea of sharing you with two other men. I want you all to myself twenty-four/seven."

"Lucky for you I'm not looking to hook up with two other men," she said cheekily. "Guess you'll have to do."

He smacked her on the hip. "Watch it."

She glanced mischievously at him. "Or what? What happens when I'm a bad girl and don't do as you tell me?"

"Depends on how badly you're *wanting* to be punished," he said dryly. "If you're yanking my chain because you want to be spanked, I'll just ignore you."

She stuck out her lip in an exaggerated pout. "You're no fun."

"Not to worry," he said lazily. "I'll find plenty of reasons to spank that pretty ass, none of which have a damn thing to do with punishment. Remember I talked about the things I do solely for my pleasure and not yours? Seeing my mark on your sweet little behind is an example. Right before I fuck it."

She trembled again and her nipples hardened against his chest. He smiled. Somehow he imagined that he wouldn't be the only one who got pleasure from spanking her.

Chapter Fifteen

"I have a present for you," Max said.

Callie was sucking air through her nostrils, so turned on that she shook in Max's arms. And now he casually changed the subject. She wanted to growl in frustration.

But still, mention of a present perked her up.

"I'll admit up front that it's as much a present for me as it is for you."

She arched an eyebrow and leveled her stare at him. "Oh?"

He smiled and then carried her over to the couch. "Wait right here while I get it."

She watched as he rummaged in the bags that had been delivered earlier. He pulled out a white, nondescript box and carried it back to where she sat.

He settled beside her and opened the box. She frowned when she saw black material. Clothes? Hadn't he just said he wanted her naked?

But when he pulled it out, it was apparent it wasn't any sort of clothing she was familiar with. It looked like half a corset.

"Stand up," he directed as he unfolded the item.

She rose and stood before him.

"Turn around."

Dutifully she turned until her back was presented to him. She heard him shove off the couch and the next thing she knew, he reached around her and positioned the wide band of material over her waist.

Maybe it was a corset. It was soft but stiff, like the material covered a harder object. But it was flexible and wrapped around to secure in the back.

He adjusted and pulled until it rested just below her breasts and fit snugly about her waist. She looked down, still unsure of what it was or what purpose it served.

She soon had her answer.

Gently he pulled one arm behind her and bent her elbow so that her wrist lay flush against her back. She jumped when a band wrapped around her wrist, securing it to the contraption she wore.

Her pulse leapt and sped up as he pulled her other arm and secured it in the same fashion.

"Turn around."

Slowly she turned and realized that the way her arms were confined by the apparatus forced her chest forward.

"Very beautiful. I think I'd like you in this when we eat so you're completely dependent on my hand to feed you."

Her cheeks grew warm under his scrutiny. She rolled up on the balls of her feet but then flushed harder when she saw his gaze tracked the bounce of her breasts.

He lowered his head, and she closed her eyes just as his tongue flicked out and licked her nipple.

Desire crashed through her, jolting her senses into instant awareness. It was like being hit by a bus.

She was vulnerable in this position. Was it a test? Or was

he simply trying to rebuild her trust? She wasn't sure she liked being pushed. Or was he simply enjoying what he'd been so straightforward in saying he wanted?

Slowly he straightened, his brows drawn together as he studied her expression.

"What are you thinking?" he asked quietly.

She shivered under his scrutiny and swallowed nervously. Before, she would have thought nothing of letting him have it with both barrels. She'd never had any problem with speaking her mind. But now, she wasn't in a position of equality.

She licked her lips and forced herself to meet his eyes.

"Is this a test?"

He frowned and confusion—genuine confusion—clouded his eyes. No, it obviously wasn't a test and now she'd stepped into it all over again. If it *had* been a test of her trust, she'd failed miserably.

Without a word he reached round her and set her wrists free. He pulled at the material until she heard the sound of Velcro separating. It slid from her waist and he tossed it aside.

Then he turned and walked out of the living room, leaving her alone and naked.

She trembled, suddenly cold. Silence crept around her until it was heavy against her ears. She became aware of each breath until she purposely lowered her respirations so the sound wasn't so explosive in the quiet.

She'd hurt him. It hadn't been intentional. It wasn't some vindictive payback to make him suffer. But the truth was there for the both of them to see. She didn't trust him anymore. Not completely.

Hadn't she wanted him to feel at least one-quarter of the pain she'd felt when he'd left her? Hadn't she wanted to get back at him even just a little?

She had, if she was honest, but now the victory—if it could be called that—was hollow and unsatisfying. She wanted to cry, not for all the pain she'd endured but for something beautiful that was lost.

Her shoulders sagging, she turned and walked slowly to the couch where she sank into the cushions. But the leather that had felt warm and comforting before was now cold and unwelcoming.

She pulled the thin blanket around her body and up to her chin. She wouldn't cry. Not now. She'd managed to go a long time without tears.

Her eyelids drooped and she nestled her head against the arm of the sofa. Her heart ached, but it went even deeper. Soul deep.

Now that she'd actually hurt Max, she realized she didn't have the stomach for revenge. Unintentional or not, she knew that she'd suffer just as much as he would.

She wanted him back. Wanted his hands on her. His mouth. She wanted him to smile at her. She wanted him to *love* her.

When Callie awoke, she lay still a moment and stared dully toward the fireplace. The hearth looked cold and empty. Pretty symbolic.

She stirred and twisted the kink from her neck. When she stared down the couch, she saw Max sitting at the end, his gaze fixed on her.

"Max."

She hastily sat up and the blanket fell to her waist.

He cocked his head to the side as his stare slid down her body. "Why didn't you dress?"

She glanced down, frowned and then looked back up at him. "You told me to stay naked."

"Hmmm."

"What's that supposed to mean?"

Okay, she sounded defensive. Hell, she *was* defensive. She was seriously teetering here and definitely working without a safety net.

"Just that on some level you trust me. I haven't completely lost it."

She sighed. "I'm so sorry, Max. I didn't mean to make you feel bad."

He scooted forward on the couch and put a finger to her mouth. "Shhh. You won't apologize for the way you feel. It's my fault. I pushed too hard, too fast. It's easy to forget that we've been apart for so many months. I'd love nothing more than to forget it and go back to the way things were before... Before I hurt you. That's on me, though. I can't expect to gain back everything we lost in a day. So it's me who is sorry, Callie. Your hesitation hurt me more than I expected. I can't bear the thought that you'd worry I'd in some way hurt you."

She leaned forward until her forehead rested on his mouth. "I don't think you'd hurt me, Max. I don't. I want this to work."

He laid his hand on the back of her head and then gently stroked over her hair as he kissed her forehead.

"I want this to work too, Callie. I shouldn't have reacted as I did. You have the *right* to question me. You have the right to stop me at any time if you don't feel comfortable. I don't want you to feel like you ever have to suck it up and deal when you're frightened or unsure just because you don't want to hurt my feelings."

She closed her eyes and smiled as she circled his neck with her arms. "I really didn't mean to hurt you, Max. I guess you're right. I'm just a little unsure. I'm still unbalanced by it all. A few days ago I was alone and unhappy. Now such a short time later, I'm with you in Denver and we're flying into the wind again."

He cupped her face and brushed his lips across her cheek and then pulled her against him to cradle her in his arms.

"I'm sorry, *dolcezza*," he murmured against her hair. "I'm sorry I hurt you. I'm sorry I overreacted earlier."

She snuggled against his chest. "Think we could take up where we left off?"

He chuckled softly. "I can arrange that."

She slid off his lap and went to her knees in front of him. She eased her thighs apart and slowly turned her hands palms up on top of her thighs.

His nostrils flared with his quick intake of breath. "How beautiful you are, Callie. There on your knees, your eyes and mouth so sweet you take my breath away."

She stared back at him, her heart squeezing so hard in her chest she became light-headed. She put all her conviction into her gaze, her expression, the position of her body. She wanted there to be no doubt. She was his. This time... This time would be right. This time would be different.

For the first time since Max had stormed back into her life she didn't feel foolish for thinking that things could be worked out between them. She was able to look at him with love, and in time she knew that her trust would be complete and whole again.

Maybe not overnight, but it would come.

She had faith.

She had love.

She had...*hope.* Sweet, healing hope.

Chapter Sixteen

Max absorbed the love in Callie's eyes like a man dying of thirst. She was a balm to every ache in his soul. He wanted to possess her. He wanted to own her. He wanted her to light up for him—only him.

But he also wanted her to be free. He never wanted to crush her spirit and the zest with which she embraced life.

She was special.

She was his.

He rose to stand before her and stared down as she looked up into his eyes. They burned with trust where before there had been a subtle wariness to her gaze. He knew he wasn't completely there yet, but she *wanted* to trust him and that was a huge step forward.

Slowly he undid the fly of his pants and pushed them over his hips until his cock jutted free of confinement. He wrapped his hand around the base and gave a short pull but then squeezed the tip when he found just how precariously close he was to coming undone under the caress of her gaze.

Holding his cock, he guided it toward her mouth.

"Open."

Her mouth slowly opened, and she licked over her lips before opening wider with a breathy little sigh that had him itching to bury himself as fast and as deep as he could.

His hand shook and the head of his dick bumped clumsily against her lips as he guided it into the hot velvet of her mouth.

Pleasure exploded over his body. His muscles jerked and his knees nearly buckled as she sucked wetly while he pushed further inside. She was a craving like he'd never experienced. Edgy. Nearly painful. His skin was uncomfortable, like he needed to shed it. Itchy. Alive. Hot.

Need. It burned through his veins like feathers tinged with acid. It was soft but sharp. Pleasure mixed with pain. Satisfaction mixed with mounting impatience.

"Hands behind your back."

He wanted to see her up on her knees, her breasts pushed forward.

She readily complied, pushing herself upward as she looped her arms bchind her.

"Now tilt your head back. Just a little. Perfect, *dolcezza*. Just like that."

Now he could see her throat bulge and work up and down as the angle sent him dccper into her mouth. It was an erotic sight, such a sweet mouth and eyes.

He reached down and stroked the sides of her neck, marveling at the baby-soft skin. The muscles jumped and quivered as he stroked to the back of her throat. He held himself there for a long moment, liking how her neck and shoulders tensed.

Through it all she never protested. Never asked him to stop. Calm acceptance blanketed them both. It was like a beautiful classical piece played to perfection.

He eased back, allowing her to breathe and relax for a moment. He was tuned in to her body. Knew the exact moment she needed a reprieve. Knew when she wanted more and when he should back off.

It had always been like this. He'd been able to read her mind and body from the start. They'd been in perfect harmony. A perfect match.

Until he'd walked away.

Until he'd had doubts that he could go through with the reason he'd sought her out.

He pulled back quickly as he realized he'd pushed too far as darker thoughts intruded into the moment. She breathed hard through her nose, and he pulled all the way out of her mouth, pissed that he'd allowed himself to become distracted even for a moment.

"Will you allow me to put your present back on you?" he asked as he stroked his erection with one hand.

She nodded without hesitation and he smiled his approval.

He extended his hand down to her, and she slid her slender fingers over his palm as he pulled her to stand before him.

He retrieved the waist restraint from the end of the couch and wrapped it around her, securing it in the back. Then he pulled her arms back and cuffed her wrists.

"Come over to the chair," he said as he directed her toward the large ottoman situated in front of the overstuffed leather chair catty-corner to the couch.

"On the ottoman. On your knees."

When she positioned herself according to his wishes, he gently lowered her head until her cheek rested on the edge of the chair. He then spread her knees so that she was open to him and he got a prime view of the soft pink flesh of her pussy and the puckered rosette of her anal opening.

"Beautiful. So pretty and so feminine."

He ran a finger through the silken, damp flesh and teased her opening before going lower to dance over the taut bud of her clitoris. Her entire body tensed and her knees shook.

He smiled. So responsive. So fucking beautiful she made his teeth ache.

"Be right back, *dolcezza.* Don't move that pretty ass. I'm going to fuck it."

He grinned again when a violent shudder rolled through her body. He slid his fingers through her pussy once more before he backed away, delighted that she'd grown even wetter at his husky promise.

He strode from the room but took his time locating the lubricant from his bathroom. He wanted her to kneel there and anticipate the moment when he'd come back. When he'd fight her resisting opening to push inside her gorgeous ass and the indescribable sensation when her body surrendered and allowed him entry.

Christ but he was hard as a rock at the image—from the *memory*—of how it felt.

There was nothing better than a slow, sensual fuck inside her ass. Drawing out both their pleasure. Opening her, then pulling out before pushing back in to reopen her all over again.

He closed his eyes and palmed his aching cock as he walked back into the living room. When he opened them and saw her where he'd left her, ass perched delectably in the air, it was all he could do to breathe.

When he went back to her, the sight of her soft pink folds was more than he could take. Holding the lubricant in one hand, he guided his cock into her pussy with the other.

She sighed and tightened around him, her pussy gripping his dick like a fist. For a moment he simply closed his eyes and slid back and forth through her velvet heat.

Buried to the hilt, he uncapped the lubricant and used his fingers to spread her cheeks so that her opening was bared. He squeezed a generous amount of the gel over the seam of her ass and then ran his thumb over the puckered rosette.

He was patient, sliding one finger through the tight opening. She clenched around him and he heard her breath hiss from her lips. Back and forth, slowly, he tucked his finger into her before finally adding a second.

He curled his other hand around the base of his cock and slowly withdrew from her pussy and positioned the head at her lubricated entrance.

She posed an erotic picture, ass stuck in the air, her hands secured helplessly around her back and her cheek pressed into the cushion of the chair. There wasn't a part of her body that wasn't open and accessible to him.

Carefully he pushed forward, forcing the broad crown of his penis into her tiny opening. The sensation of the tight ring squeezing his erection nearly sent him over the edge. She sheathed him with unbearable tightness.

She opened around him, but her body fought his invasion. He pressed forward relentlessly, not giving an inch as he forced more of his length into her ass.

With a slight plop, the head pushed through, and she gasped and wiggled beneath him.

"Too much?"

"No," she whispered hoarsely. "Not enough. Never enough."

In response, he pushed hard, forcing another inch inside her.

He was lodged halfway in her. The sight of him piercing the opening between her cheeks sent his pulse skyrocketing. It didn't seem possible that he could fit into her body this way, but he knew not only was it possible, but that she had accommodated him easily. Many, many times.

He withdrew a few centimeters and then gripped her hips, holding her steady, and thrust hard.

He sank into her body, his cock sliding through the tight opening until his hips met the curve of her buttocks. His balls pressed against her pussy and he rotated, rubbing his sac over the softness of her entrance.

"You feel so damn good, *dolcezza*," he groaned. "I've dreamed of reclaiming your body. Of reclaiming what's mine."

He remained still a moment longer and then gently withdrew, watching his cock reappear as her opening stretched and widened around him.

When only the tip remained inside her entrance, he pushed forward again, watching once more as her body gave him access.

He pressed into her ass, rocking his hips against her lush bottom. He closed his eyes and rubbed up and down and then side to side, relearning her body, straining to go deeper, to the very heart of her.

He took his time, making love to her as sweetly as if he were sliding into her warm pussy. His fingers dug into her hips, holding her tightly so that he could push into her each time he withdrew.

Finally he reached underneath and slid his hands down the tops of her thighs until he pushed at her knees to cause her to go down on her belly.

No longer supported by her legs, she lay flat over the ottoman with him pressed to her body as his hips worked against her ass.

He kissed her shoulder then nipped at the flesh with his

teeth. He loved marking her. Loved leaving little reminders of his possession. He sucked sharply at the curve of her neck until he left a light red welt that faded slightly when he pulled away.

"My *dolcezza.*"

He arched off her and carefully withdrew. He spread her buttocks so that he could see the enlarged and slightly reddened opening that his cock had just come from. Keeping her wide, he flexed his hips so that his cock lodged inside her opening again and he pushed forward.

Then he withdrew, holding her open again as he stared down, watching as her body slowly closed. He positioned himself again and then thrust hard, eliciting a gasp from her as she wiggled under his forceful lunge.

He kept her pinned to the ottoman, satisfaction tightening every muscle in his body. His. She belonged to him. She was his to do with as he wished.

He flexed again and a shudder of pleasure shook through his body until he sucked air violently through his nose in an effort to control himself.

He began pumping with quick, short motions, closing his eyes as his balls drew up into hard knots. He kept his hands on her cheeks until he was sure she'd wear his fingerprints on her flesh. He squeezed, kneaded and then spread her wider, wanting her completely open to him when he shot semen over and inside her ass.

Her fingers curled into tight little balls at the small of her back. He gripped her harder as he slowly began to unravel.

Threads of silk surrounding his heart popped and frayed as his chest swelled with emotion. She undid him. Always had. No one could make him lose control like she did. He alternately loved and hated her for that.

He was barely rimming her entrance now as he continued

to thrust fast and furious. Still holding her cheek in one hand, he reached frantically for his cock with the other and began jerking as he aimed at her opening.

The first rope of semen splashed inside her and then a second until the thick, white cream filled the opening and trailed down the inside of her leg.

He groaned with each pull and more liquid splashed onto her ass and into the wide-open entrance. He loved filling her, opening her to him, marking her in the most primitive way a man could mark a woman.

He guided more onto her behind and over her fists secured to her back. Her ass glistened with shiny fluid that trailed down the backs of her thighs.

Then he guided his erection back into her opening, sliding all the way in with one push. He closed his eyes as the last of his release spilled inside her. For a long moment he held himself still, simply enjoying the sensation of being seated so deep inside her body. Then slowly he withdrew.

He backed away, staring down at her with satisfaction.

Quietly he walked back to the bathroom where he spent a few moments cleaning up, and then he wet a washcloth with warm water and returned to Callie where she still lay awaiting his next command.

Gently, he cleaned her, wiping the trails of semen from her skin. Then he reached up to unfasten her hands and let them fall limply at her sides.

Then he helped her sit up and pulled her into his arms. Lifting her effortlessly, he carried her over to the couch where he sat and cuddled her against his chest.

"I didn't hurt you, did I?"

She shook her head against his shoulder.

"You have a sweet ass, Callie. I love fucking it. There isn't a part of your delectable body that I don't love fucking."

She yawned tiredly but when she looked up, her eyes shone and sparkled like they hadn't since he'd returned. He touched her cheek and then leaned forward to kiss each eyelid.

"Do you need the bathroom?"

She nodded and he carefully rose, still holding her tight against him. He carried her into the bathroom and set her down, holding onto her until he was sure her legs were sturdy enough that she wouldn't fall.

"Okay?"

She smiled and turned away. While he waited, he turned on the shower to warm the water.

A few moments later, she returned, and he pulled her into the stall and under the spray with him.

With gentle hands, he washed her body, paying special attention to the areas he was hardest on. She was warm and sleek in his hands. And so very willing.

He scraped his mouth across the mark on her neck, and then he lapped it with his tongue. "You'll wear many reminders of my possession tomorrow."

She smiled and arched her back, the spray bouncing off her breasts and belly as she reached to curl her arms around him.

"I can still feel your marks," she murmured. "Your fingers on my skin. Your mouth on my neck. I'll go to sleep tonight remembering what you felt like."

His body tightened at the sultry, seductive words.

"You'll go to sleep tonight *feeling* me, not remembering me," he corrected.

Her smile grew broader, and she rolled up on the balls of

her feet so she could kiss the corner of his mouth.

"I don't think I'm going to be able to walk by the time we go back home."

He slid his hand over the curve of her behind and squeezed lightly. "If I had my way, *dolcezza,* you'd never walk again."

Chapter Seventeen

Max was awake at dawn. He'd never owned an alarm clock in his life. His internal clock had never let him down. Even with the many time zones he crossed in his travels, he had an uncanny knack for knowing what time it was and he rarely slept past sunrise.

Except for those magical days with Callie in Europe. He'd allowed himself latitude he rarely gave. He became lazy and unmotivated. Or rather his motivation changed from the moment he met her.

She was draped across him like a warm blanket, her legs tangled with his. It was a very possessive gesture. One he delighted in. He might be the more dominant one in their relationship, but she was mighty possessive of him in her own right.

He fingered a strand of her dark brown hair and listened to her inhale and exhale. Her breath blew over his neck, a sensation that pleased him.

Yes, his motivation had changed when he'd come face to face with the woman he'd tracked across three countries. A seduction and courtship that was supposed to have lasted a week had turned into three weeks he'd never forget.

Before he met Callie, his family was the single most important thing in his life. There wasn't anything he wouldn't do to take care of them, protect them, make them happy. Damn the cost or consequences.

Callie had changed all of that.

How could he keep his promise to his family and his promise to Callie that he'd never hurt her? The simple answer was that he couldn't, and he'd known it from the beginning. He'd chosen Callie. His promise would go unfulfilled, and he was making his peace with that choice.

His gut twisted and some of his satisfaction melted away. He couldn't change the past or what his primary motivation had been when he'd made sure his and Callie's paths crossed, but he could make sure she never found out. What mattered was what his motivation was going forward.

She stirred against him, and he tightened his hold on her, simply wanting the reassurance of her warmth. She raised her head and stared at him with sleepy, contented eyes.

"Good morning," she said on a sigh.

He kissed her. More savagely than the moment called for, but some of the darkness still hadn't receded.

She went soft against him, accepting the carnal heat of his mouth. He rolled her underneath him, his knee between her thighs. With a quick nudge, she was open and accessible. He was inside her before he took his next breath.

He was instantly at peace. She did this to him—for him. For a long moment he remained lodged within her, staring down into her eyes, absorbing her acceptance. Soaking in her love.

She raised her hands and cupped his face then stroked lightly over his cheekbones as if to tell him everything would be all right. As if she knew the dark turn of his thoughts.

He closed his eyes and took in deep breaths as her fingers stroked over his face. Then he turned so her hand slid over his mouth and he kissed the inside of her palm.

She pulsed around him, her heat surrounding him, inviting him deeper—into the very heart of her soul. He withdrew slowly, opening his eyes to watch the play of emotions dance across her face.

Her eyes darkened, and she sucked in a quick breath as he pushed forward again.

He'd fully intended it to be a quick, rough fuck. He'd wanted to take. To be selfish. But now as he watched her, he tempered his movements, going slow and more gently than he imagined he could.

He wanted to wrap her in silk, protect her from every bad thing in the world—including himself.

Slowly, he lowered his mouth to hers and kissed her with all the tenderness he was capable of.

"I'm sorry," he murmured even as he pushed inside her again. "I was rough with you last night. I should have been more careful this morning. You must be sore."

She smiled and curled her arms around his neck. She kissed him sweetly, covering each tiny part of his mouth before sliding to his jaw and then to his ear.

He shivered as she nipped delicately at his lobe and then sucked it between her teeth.

"I'm okay," she whispered into his ear. "I love waking to you inside me. It's a beautiful way of reminding me I belong to you."

Dear God. Her words slid over his skin and soaked deep into his heart. His chest ached and became so heavy he could barely breathe.

"I love...you," he said in a voice he didn't recognize. "Just you."

Her eyes widened in shock and then filled with tears. The

sight nearly undid him. How could she be so surprised? Had he held back so much? Had she doubted... Stupid question. Of course she had. He hadn't given her any reason to believe she was anything but a holiday fling.

How he hated what he'd done to her confidence. And he'd done nothing to allay those fears when he'd returned. He hadn't come back and said, "I love you." He'd come back and said, "I want you."

He kissed away the tear that slid over her cheek. "I do love you, *dolcezza*. I'm sorry this is the first time you've heard the words. I'm sorry that this is the first time I've given them to you."

She squeezed him and lifted her hips to take more of him. So characteristic of her. Always giving. Always willing to take more from him.

"I only care that you've said them," she said in an aching voice. "I love you too, Max. So much. I've missed you..."

She broke off as another silver trail slid over her cheek. He hushed her with another kiss. "I missed you too, Callie. Never doubt it. Say it again. Let me have the words again."

"I love you."

He'd never considered himself an overly emotional man. He was always in complete control of himself and his actions—his reactions. But Callie... That she loved him, that she was willing to forgive, willing to give of herself so freely after the way he'd hurt her.

The knot grew more uncomfortable in his throat. He kissed her again, not knowing what else to do. He couldn't speak. He didn't trust himself not to give way to the building tide of emotion in his chest.

Thank God. Thank God she still loved him. That she wasn't holding back after all he'd done. He couldn't—wouldn't allow her to know just how far he'd been willing to go to keep a promise to his family. It would destroy her.

"Are you with me, *dolcezza*? Are you close? Tell me what you need."

She sighed again and her smile was so dazzling that it spilled sunshine all over him.

"You, Max. Just you. Love me. I'm always with you."

Her words unleashed his tightly held control. He thrust deep and started coming before he was even at full depth. She arched into his arms and wrapped her legs tightly around his, their bodies woven together in a beautiful tapestry.

Max and Callie. Callie and Max.

She buried her face in his neck and then sank her teeth into the column of his throat as she came apart. Her body tugged relentlessly at him, pulling him deeper, and then went liquid around him, bathing him in intense, sweet heat.

For the longest time he lay atop her, their legs and bodies meshed together as he pulsed inside her. It was hard not to imagine his seed taking root. For a moment he fantasized about her big and round with his child.

He wanted these things. He wanted her unreservedly. Her submission, her love. He wanted all of her. He wanted children. Lots of girls with her indomitable spirit, her sassy smile and those gorgeous blue eyes. He wanted boys who were as strong and as resilient as she was.

"Are you still on birth control?" he asked a moment later.

"Yes."

He couldn't help the stark disappointment that surged through his body.

She pulled away, a frown curving her mouth downward. "Why?"

He smiled then, wanting to ease her worry and not put a damper on what was otherwise an incredible moment for him.

"I just had this image of you. Pregnant with my child. Of feeling your belly, big and round. I liked it. I liked it a lot."

She relaxed and then grinned. "You're going to have to wait a while for that, I'm afraid. I have way too much I want to do and see before I start popping out a brood of children."

He lifted an eyebrow. "A brood?" He was teasing her, because suddenly the idea of being surrounded by a pile of kids was completely pleasing to him.

"I always imagined that I'd have a lot of children," she said wistfully. "Eventually. Not right away. But when I was ready. I love having a large family. I loved growing up with three older brothers."

He pushed himself up and off of her, carefully withdrawing from the delicious heat of her body. He settled beside her and pulled her into his arms until their noses nearly touched.

"Tell me of all these things you want to do before you settle down and have babies."

She snuggled against him until their legs were once more entwined.

"I love to travel. I like to just...go. Whenever I get the urge. My mom has always said I was born with my head in the clouds and my eyes always looking toward a place I'd never been. She's probably right. I have wanderlust. There's nothing quite like just packing up and going. Seeing new places, meeting new people, seeing the sun rise and set in a different place each day."

"I want to show you those places. I want to see them with you. I'll show you the world, Callie."

Her eyes shone and glistened again, but he was determined

not to make her cry. No more. He wanted to make her happy.

"I love you, Max. So much."

Would he ever grow tired of hearing those words? He couldn't imagine such a thing. If anything, he worried she'd grow tired of his need to hear them.

"I love you, *dolcezza*. I need you to know that."

She smiled. "I do now."

He kissed her again, long and leisurely, as he should have done earlier when she was just awakening. He apologized now as he gently fed at her lips and savored each touch and taste.

And then he held her, until the soft even tempo of her breathing signaled that she'd drifted back to sleep. He smiled and slid his leg more firmly over hers, until her body was completely sheltered by his. Shopping could wait.

Chapter Eighteen

Shopping with Max was a decadent experience. Callie loved to shop. She had all her girly tendencies intact. But shopping with Max?

From the time they walked into the upscale stores, Callie was pampered, catered to, fawned over and draped from head to toe with beautiful, expensive clothing.

Through it all, Max kept a close watch. He never seemed to tire as Callie tried on outfit after outfit. He'd stand back and study for a moment before simply nodding or shaking his head, and then the salesperson would hurriedly divest Callie of the outfit and either toss it in the discard pile or whisk it away to the to-be-bought pile.

And he had impeccable taste. He knew exactly what looked good on her, what flattered her and what didn't. No expense was spared.

He even insisted she model the lingerie he chose, although he was very clear that no one but he got to see those particular modeling sessions.

She felt…beautiful. A little devilish and very sexy. She watched his eyes, saw the way he looked at her, and she ate every single moment up.

She loved being spoiled by Max. She'd gotten a taste of it in Europe, but now that he'd made his feelings clear for her, his lavish treatment took on a more endearing quality.

Behind the dressing screen, she grinned as she pulled on a particularly scanty pair of panties and a matching bra. They didn't leave much to the imagination, and the panties...had a little surprise that she was eager to show Max.

She poked her head out and his gaze immediately fixed on her. Then she shyly stepped out in the daring high heels she'd donned just for this outfit.

His eye smoldered dark as his gaze traveled up and down her body. She strutted forward and straddled his lap until he was forced to lean his head back to look into her eyes.

Emboldened by his response, she reached for the fly of his pants and slid her hand inside as she unzipped him. His cock jumped in response when her fingers curled around his length.

"What are you doing, you little minx?"

Continuing to caress him, she leaned down and took his mouth with hers, kissing him until they were both struggling for breath.

"You asked for a private lingerie showing. I intend to show you just how this particular lingerie works."

Before he could respond, she arched over him and fit the head of his cock through the slit in her underwear. He sucked in his breath in surprise as he slid through the material and deep into her wetness.

"Holy shit. I'm buying you these in every color they have."

She grinned, adjusted her position and then sank down until she'd sheathed his entire length. He curled his hands around her hips to keep her in place and nuzzled the lacy edge of her bra until he had the cup worked down enough that her nipple poked over the top.

He licked the rigid peak, coaxing it even tighter. Her head

fell back and she closed her eyes as pleasure shot through her veins. Up and down she bounced on his lap, aided by his hands still dug into her hips.

The sheer naughtiness of having sex in a department store fueled her desire to greater heights. She felt incredibly sexy, daring, a vixen bent on pleasuring her man.

Her head swung back down, and she fixed her stare to his as he pulled slowly away from her breast.

"You are a deviant, naughty temptress," he ground out.

She lifted her behind from his lap and then slowly lowered herself back down his length until he was buried to the balls.

"You say that like they're bad qualities," she said mischievously.

"Oh hell no. You were already my dream girl. Today just cements it. I love every deviant bone in your body. Now I wonder how loud I can make you scream."

The wicked gleam in his eyes told her he'd have no qualms about doing just that. Okay, so she might not mind being a naughty girl when she knew no one was looking, but it didn't mean she was ready to let the entire store know that she and Max were fucking like bunnies behind a curtain.

He chuckled low. "I'm teasing you, *dolcezza.*"

He lifted her up and motioned for her to stand. Confused, she did as he gestured and waited for what he wanted.

He made a circling motion with his hand and she turned until her back was to him. Then he gripped her waist and guided her back toward his straining cock.

"Lean forward."

As she did his bidding, his hands left her waist and smoothed over her back, up her spine to her hair. Then he slowly worked back down, over her ass and to the slit in the crotch of her underwear.

His finger eased inside her and her knees buckled. She would have pitched forward but he caught her with one hand. The head of his penis brushed through the underwear but instead of finding her entrance, it brushed over her clit.

He rubbed back and forth from her quivering bud to her entrance and then back until she was slick and wet and so very ready to have him back inside her.

She tried to take matters into her hands by pushing back when he rubbed around her opening. His response was to smack her loudly on the ass.

She jumped, more startled than pained. All too soon the burn turned to a low hum of pleasure that worked over her behind and had her squirming for more.

"Sit back now."

Eager to do his bidding, she sat and closed her eyes as his length slid easily into her pussy.

"Now work it. Fuck me. But watch yourself in the mirror as you do."

She gasped. She'd forgotten about the triple mirror just in front of her. Now that her gaze lifted and focused on her reflection, she was transfixed by the naughty vixen staring back at her.

Her breasts spilled from the dainty bra. Her legs were spread and she could see the mesh of flesh where she and Max were joined.

Her cheeks were flushed and her eyes gleamed. Her hair... Her hair was tousled and mussed, her lips swollen. She looked like a woman well loved.

She pulled forward just enough that his cock slid back almost out of her pussy. Mesmerized by the picture they presented, she slammed back, moaning at the instant sense of fullness.

"Cup your breasts. Roll your nipples and let me watch you in the mirror."

She straightened enough that he had a good view and then reached into the cups of her bra and lifted until her breasts came free.

He wrapped his hands back around her hips and took over directing her movements while she pinched and rolled her nipples between her thumb and fingers.

"You look beautiful. Wild and wanton. My sweet vixen."

She stared back at herself, saw Max watching around her shoulder as he pulled her down on him over and over. She felt beautiful. And as he'd said, wanton. Wild. Bold.

"Keep touching yourself. I'll take care of the rest."

Raw need rolled over her. Hot and edgy. Her skin prickled. Her orgasm bloomed, swelling until she fidgeted restlessly in his grasp.

Her breasts, so much more sensitive now, felt heavy in her palms. Each brush of her fingers across her nipples sent shard after shard of ecstasy streaking through her abdomen and lower until she convulsed hotly around his cock.

"Use your fingers on your clit. Come when I come, *dolcezza.*"

Leaving one of her breasts, she sucked her finger into her mouth until it was damp. Then she slowly trailed it down her midline, over her belly and underneath the lace of her panties until she delved into her folds to find her swollen, super-sensitized clit.

As soon as she rolled her finger over the tiny nub of flesh, her entire body clenched painfully. He thrust harder, his grip tightening at her hips.

She tried to call back the moan that welled in her throat but it came out in a low, husky hum.

"That's it, baby. Come for me. I'm so close."

He was so tight inside her, so swollen and rigid that it became harder for him to thrust. Each movement sent her spiraling ever nearer to release.

She gasped when he withdrew and plunged—hard—sending him to greater depths. There was an edgy mixture of pain and mind-bending pleasure that left her insides clawing to be set free.

And then she simply catapulted forward. The excruciating tension broke, sending her into a million tiny pieces. A rainbow of color flashed in her vision and her reflected image blurred as he pumped harder and harder into her.

With a growl he slammed her back onto his lap and held onto her so fiercely that his fingers left impressions in her skin. He flooded hot and hard into her clenching womb. She fell back into him, suddenly exhausted and limp.

Max collected her into his arms, her back pressed to his chest. He turned her face toward him and nuzzled her cheek as he whispered over and over that he loved her.

Drowsily she opened her eyes to see herself in the mirror. Sprawled indelicately across Max's lap, his cock trapped between her legs. She was wet and sticky, and she glanced ruefully down at the very expensive panties they'd just ruined.

"Guess you'll be buying these for sure."

He chuckled and nibbled affectionately at her shoulder. "These and a dozen others."

She tried to stand but teetered on the ridiculous heels she'd slipped on. Her legs were as shaky as a newborn colt's.

Max caught her before she could pitch forward and then he rose.

"Get cleaned up and changed. I'll take care of getting your clothing together. Oh, and wear one of those pairs of underwear out of the store with the red skirt we chose and the silk top."

"I'm going to freeze!" she protested.

The corner of his mouth lifted into a smile. "I'll keep you warm, *dolcezza*."

Chapter Nineteen

Callie felt conspicuous as they left the store and Max tucked her into the backseat of his car. It was silly. No one knew what she had on underneath her skirt. The underwear was perfectly respectable...except for the sly little gap that made her pussy accessible.

Max gave the driver instructions, although Callie didn't much pay attention to where they were going. Then Max turned his attention to her and pulled her onto his lap so that she sat sideways across him.

The flat of his palm rested on her knee and he pushed higher, taking the filmy material of her skirt with him. She sucked in her breath and cast a nervous glance in the driver's direction, but the privacy glass was up. He couldn't see back here, could he?

She promptly forgot all about her concerns when Max's fingers dipped past the slit in her underwear and found her damp heat.

She'd just had the orgasm to end all orgasms and yet when he touched her, her body leapt to instant and aching awareness.

"You're playful today, *dolcezza*. And very, very naughty. I'll have to come up with a suitable punishment for your wanton behavior."

Her eyes widened and she stared incredulously at him. "Punishment? You ought to be thanking me. What guy wouldn't like for a woman to fuck his brains out during a lingerie show? Why on earth would you punish me?"

He smiled. "Because it suits me?"

Ah, the answer to everything in Max's world. Because it suited him. She should have remembered that his punishments had little to do with actual infractions and more to do with his whims. Not that she minded.

Still, she turned her bottom lip down into a pouty sulk, because she also knew he loved it when she pouted.

He leaned up, caught her bottom lip between his teeth and sucked it into his mouth. "Such a pretty pout. I'll have to punish you for that too."

She rolled her eyes but squeezed them shut when he slid two fingers into her pussy. He continued to play as they rolled down the avenue. Forgotten was her complaint that she'd freeze in her current apparel. She was flushed from head to toe as he worked his magic. He was patient. Very exacting. Working her to the point of orgasm and then stopping until she came down from the verge.

Then he'd begin again until she was crazy with wanting. His thumb stroked gently over her clit as his fingers explored her swollen tissues. He added a third finger and she arched, knowing that if he didn't stop at this precise point, she'd come.

Only he did.

He laughed softly at her expression. She could only imagine how frustrated she looked. She wanted to pounce on him and fuck his brains out all over again, and she couldn't care less whether the driver saw and heard.

"Would you like to come?"

"Yes!" she hissed.

Slowly he withdrew his fingers, and then he licked each one, sucking her moisture from the tips, all the while staring at her.

"I want you hungry. I want you on edge. I plan to keep you there all afternoon. Then I'm going to take you home and spank that pretty ass of yours until you're begging me to take you. Then and only then am I going to fuck you. It won't be easy, *dolcezza.* I'm going to own you. It won't be a nice, easy taking. You'll have no doubt as to my possession. I'm going to fuck that sultry mouth of yours. I'm going to fuck you here." He slid his fingers between her legs again and opened her as he ran a finger around her entrance. "And I'm going to fuck that delectable ass of yours and then I'm going to come all over you. Then I think I'll spank you all over again."

She quivered from head to toe. Heat rushed over her skin until she felt faint. She wavered in his grasp, bobbling like a tipsy party girl. She couldn't speak, couldn't respond to the vivid images bombarding her brain.

Suddenly there was nothing more she wanted to do than to go home and allow him to do as he pleased. And damn the man, but he knew it. The satisfied, predatory smile on his face spoke volumes. He knew precisely what he was doing to her and he loved every minute.

She sagged against him and tucked her head underneath his chin as she stared out the window at passing traffic. "You are an evil, evil man, Max Wilder. Damn if I don't love you anyway."

He chuckled. "You love me because I'm evil, and you are my match, *dolcezza.* You are every bit as evil as I am. I love that about you."

She raised her head and stared back at him, all teasing

gone. "I'm just happy that you love me."

He stared at her a long moment before sliding his hand over her cheek and then upward into her hair. He gathered the strands tight into his fist and pulled her toward his mouth to take her in a savage, demanding kiss.

For several seconds, she could barely breathe as he ravaged her lips, took possession of her mouth and tasted every inch of it.

As he pulled away, his eyes darkened with intensity. "Never doubt my love for you, Callie."

"I won't," she said softly. "Not now."

"Not ever."

She nodded.

Max glanced ahead and then carefully arranged her skirt so that she was covered. "We're here."

She slid off his lap onto the seat and finished arranging her clothing so that she was presentable. "Where's here?"

He smiled. "You'll see."

The driver opened the door and Max stepped out. He reached back to take Callie's hand and helped her onto the sidewalk. She blinked to try and clear the cobwebs that were muddying her mind. That was also Max's fault. Her brain had gone to mush and now all she could think about was what was to come later.

Max pulled her into his side as a brisk wind kicked up. He hurried them toward a jewelry store two doors up. Callie recognized the name. Very exclusive. Very expensive.

It wasn't that she wasn't used to being around money. Her parents had money. It was just that Callie didn't. Not that she couldn't, but from the time she'd been old enough to understand that her parents were wealthy, she'd always been determined to pay her own way. Much to her parents' dismay.

With three fathers all dying to spoil their only little girl, Callie had put a kink in their plans by refusing to let them pay for anything.

These kinds of places made her nervous. Not that she hadn't been in them. But they made her feel like a fraud.

They went inside, and an older gentleman in an expensive suit immediately came forward to greet Max.

"Good to see you, Mr. Wilder."

Max took his outstretched hand and shook it briefly. "And you, Winston. Do you have them ready for me?"

Winston nodded and motioned for Max and Callie to follow him into a small room off the main showroom.

"Please, have a seat." He gestured toward two plush armchairs in front of a highly polished executive desk. He then walked around to sit behind the desk and he opened one of the drawers.

He drew out a velvet case, much larger than Callie would have imagined. She raised an inquisitive brow in Max's direction. He only smiled and directed Winston to open the box.

Winston complied and turned the box around, pushing it in Max's direction.

Inside were two intricately designed bracelets. Although they were much wider than a typical bracelet. They looked more like cuffs.

Max pulled one of the pieces of jewelry out of the box and held it up. He looked at it from side to side and then made a sound of approval before picking up the second one.

"Put your arms out, *dolcezza.*"

She did so without hesitation. Max first clasped one around her left wrist and then placed the other one on her right wrist.

The cool metal closed around her flesh and to her surprise, he took out a tiny key, inserted it into the clasp and locked it.

"I considered gold, but platinum looks more beautiful on you," he said. "It suits you."

He raised both hands to view the jewelry on her wrists. Satisfaction lit his eyes and then he glanced at her. "Do you like them?"

She carefully pulled her hands away from Max so she could study the intricate designs on the bands. Along the bottom of the left cuff was inscribed: *Two halves of a whole.* She glanced at the right cuff to see inscribed: *We are one.*

And on the inside in flowery script: *Max and Callie.*

Tears shimmered in her vision and she lifted her gaze to Max. "They're beautiful."

Max raised his hand dismissively, and Winston hurried out of the office, leaving Max and Callie alone. Max returned his attention to her and gathered her hands in his.

"You'll wear these as long as we're together. You'll not take them off. Ever. We'll both have a key, but know that you voluntarily taking them off will mean that you no longer want to be with me. In my eyes these are more binding than a wedding ring. They signal my possession. My ownership and your acceptance of that. Do you understand?"

She nodded, not trusting herself to speak around the knot in her throat.

He raised her hands to his mouth and pressed a kiss across her knuckles. "I love you, Callie. This more than anything else is a symbol of that love."

She smiled brilliantly, until her cheeks ached with the effort. "I love them, Max. I'll wear them always."

His eyes lit up and his smile was as broad as hers. The joy

in his expression made her heart clench, and a giddy thrill rushed down her spine. He loved her. She made him happy. It was almost too much for her to contemplate.

"Are you hungry? It's getting late in the afternoon and I have yet to feed you. I'm neglecting my *dolcezza*."

"Starving," she admitted. "Being naughty is hard work!"

His laughter filled the room and he stood, pulling her up next to him. He caught her against him and tipped her chin up to receive his kiss. "You are so perfect for me, Callie." He squeezed her one last time and then ushered her from the office and out to the waiting car.

Chapter Twenty

On the drive back to Max's apartment, Callie battled the blanket of lethargy that settled over her. But the moment they arrived and took the lift up to his penthouse, anticipation replaced the threads of fatigue.

Her body hummed with excitement as she remembered the promises he'd made for when they returned.

The doorman accompanied them up, carrying the many bags with the extravagant purchases Max had made. Max directed him to drop them just inside the door, and then the doorman made a discreet exit, leaving Max and Callie standing in the foyer.

"You may leave your clothing here," Max said as he pointed to a coat rack and a small wicker basket placed strategically by the door.

Callie quickly undressed, hanging her shirt and skirt on the hook. She slipped off her bra and underwear and let them flutter from her fingers into the basket. When she would have discarded her heels, Max put a hand to her wrist to stop her.

"Keep the shoes. I find I quite like them on you."

She smiled. They were killer. Total fuck-me shoes. Red stilettos with three-inch heels. They complemented her legs, making them look much longer and sleeker than they were.

He gestured for her to walk ahead of him into the living room, and she set off, the heels tapping across the polished floor.

She stopped in the middle of the room, unsure of where he'd want her. She turned to find his gaze fixed solidly on her. He seemed to be contemplating... What, she wasn't sure, but it sent a trail of chill bumps over her shoulders and down to her breasts until her nipples beaded and puckered.

He smiled lazily. "I don't know whether to wait and make you anticipate what is to come or whether to give in to my own impatience and begin now."

She remained silent, watching him and waiting. She was a very impatient person—always had been—but she found with Max that she was perfectly willing to await his pleasure.

"Tell me, *dolcezza*, have I tired you out too much today? Do you need to rest for a while?"

Trust Max to be ever so considerate. He was always concerned with her needs even when they might contradict his own wants. She trembled under the steady weight of his gaze. Her body was alive with anticipation. No, she didn't need rest. She needed him.

"No," she said softly. "I need only what you want to give."

The pleasure in his eyes warmed her straight through.

"Turn around."

Slowly she turned until her back was to him. She heard him close the distance between them and then his hand cupped her behind. Lovingly he caressed, smoothing over one cheek and then the other.

She barely had time to suck in her breath before he issued a sharp blow with his palm. She jumped but he was there to steady her.

"Careful. I've asked you to remain in the heels, but I won't do so to your detriment."

A warm buzz spread over her ass as the burn faded into pleasure. He rubbed and caressed the spot he'd struck, and then he smacked her other cheek. This time she was prepared and stood her ground.

Her eyes closed as he continued to caress her throbbing buttocks. Twice more he delivered a measured smack to her ass and each time he soothed the hurt with gentle caresses.

"I love seeing the imprint of my hand on your beautiful, soft skin. I enjoy watching as the hurt turns to pleasure as your body relaxes and your breathing changes. You like the pain."

She nodded.

"You also love the pleasure."

She nodded again.

He took her elbow and guided her toward the end of the couch. "Bend over and place your hands on the cushion. Let the arm cradle your belly."

She did as he asked and settled over the end of the couch until her ass was perched high in the air.

"I'm going to start slow and work up as I see how well you tolerate the pain. I'm not going to stop until your ass is completely red and you're begging me to fuck you. Can you take it, Callie? Dare I see just how far I can push you?"

Oh yes. God yes. She was nearly panting and he hadn't even begun.

"The words, Callie. I want to hear the words."

"Please, Max. Do your worst."

He chuckled then. "You have no idea what my worst is. You aren't ready for that. But you will be."

The dark thread in his voice completely contradicted his

husky laughter. She was so on edge, so keyed up by what was to come that she could orgasm right now with only one touch. And maybe that was why he was so careful not to do so.

The first smack was light. She closed her eyes, enjoying the sensation of his palm against her flesh. He delivered another to the other cheek and she moaned.

True to his word he began slow. Measured. Never twice in the same spot. He methodically covered every inch of her ass, meting out blows with the same force.

Her mouth was open and she panted softly, wanting, needing. It was on the tip of her tongue to beg him to fuck her now, but that would only disappoint him. He wanted her to take more. A lot more. She wanted to give him what he wanted.

And she absolutely wanted to see just how much she could take before she gave in to the urge to plead.

He picked up the pace and the blows became harder and more painful. But with each one, the burn was quickly replaced by soft euphoria. Almost as if she floated out of her body on a cloud of never-ending pleasure.

She closed her eyes and sighed dreamily even as the blows came faster. Harder.

The sound of the smacks rose in the quiet room. Her entire body jiggled and lurched forward, forcing her to brace herself against the cushions.

No longer could she differentiate between the blows. It was all one hazy, edgy sensation that blended in a long trail of pain and indescribable pleasure.

She floated higher and higher. Her mind was no longer her own. All she knew was Max. Max's hand. On her body. His pleasure. His belonging. His body. Not hers. She was his.

"I wish you could see how beautiful your ass is. Rosy red.

So red that you can't tell one mark from the other. It glows. Just like you."

She moaned as he began again. Harder this time. Deliberately punishing. He was driving her further and further to her breaking point.

She bit her lip to keep from crying out. She wouldn't. Not yet.

"Give me the words," he demanded. "I won't stop until you beg me. And then I'm going to fuck you until we both drop."

It was her undoing. She opened her mouth and the words spilled out.

"Please, Max. Please. Fuck me. Take me. Make me yours. Please," she said brokenly.

He left her immediately. Before she realized he'd quit, his fingers wrapped in her hair and yanked her head to the side. She was still positioned over the arm of the couch, her ass throbbing, aching, thrust high in the air, when he gripped her hair and shoved his cock into her mouth.

As he'd promised, he wasn't gentle. He fucked her mouth as ruthlessly as he'd fucked her pussy and her ass in the past. She couldn't move, couldn't do anything but lie there, his hand twisted tight in her hair as he thrust deep to the back of her throat.

He leaned over the couch so his angle was better. His body covered her face and his hips slapped against her as he pushed into her over and over until she wasn't aware of breathing, only of receiving him.

He was exerting his dominance. There was no doubt as to what he was doing. He wasn't making love to her. He was possessing her. Showing her that she belonged to him. That her body belonged to him and he could do as he liked.

She lay there, reveling in that possession. She was more than willing for him to mark her, brand her, own her. He'd never hurt her. She knew that. He'd take her as far as she could go, but he'd stop in a heartbeat if she asked him to.

She was equally determined that those words would never pass her lips.

With a harsh groan, he jerked away, leaving her to lick her swollen lips, nearly numb from the force of his possession.

He walked behind her again and rubbed over her still-throbbing ass. She gasped when he issued several sharp blows in succession.

Only when he'd worked her back up to the haze where the line between pain and pleasure was blurred did he spread her legs wide and slam into her from behind.

It was too much. She was too on edge. As soon as his cock thrust deep into her body, her orgasm rolled over her like a tidal wave.

She cried out as her body tightened, drew up, painful in its intensity. Then as if a sharp knife cut cleanly through the taut rope holding her captive, she shattered.

She screamed, the sound sharp through the silence. Her body wasn't her own. She couldn't control her reaction, couldn't hold her release at bay.

Through it all, Max hammered relentlessly, thrusting, pushing her further and further over the precipice.

She could hear herself begging, just as he'd vowed she'd do, but she had no idea what she begged for. She pleaded, wanting more, not wanting him to stop even as her breaths tore raggedly from her nose and mouth.

She wanted all of him, everything he had to give her, whatever he chose to force her to take. She wanted it. Nothing less.

Then he tore himself from her writhing body, and she let out a whimper. She felt so empty, so desolate of his possession. She craved more. Only felt complete when he was inside her, his body a part of hers. A part of her soul.

Again, the blows rained down over her ass. Faster and more furious this time as if he was every bit as driven over the edge as she was.

She gasped. Tears slid down her cheeks. And still she wanted more.

"Please," she begged quietly, her throat raw, her voice nearly gone.

He parted her throbbing cheeks and pushed into her. No preamble. No work up. His thick length forced into her ass, and the beautiful burn was back as he struggled to make her accommodate him.

She stretched around him and she pushed back, wanting all of him. Wanting that instant moment of complete possession when her body screamed no but her heart cried yes.

His fingers gripping her aching buttocks, he shoved forward with a grunt and his balls came to rest against her pussy.

"Now, I own you, Callie," he said, his voice filled with grim satisfaction. "There isn't a part of you I don't own, that doesn't have my mark. You're mine. Tell me you belong to me. Only me."

"I'm yours," she croaked out. "Only yours, Max. Always yours. Please. Take me. I'm begging. Finish it."

He withdrew and then began a relentless assault on her senses that later she'd find no comparison for. He fucked her brutally for what seemed like forever. She lay there, submissively, taking what he meted out, never wanting it to end.

In and out, his erection so much harder and thicker than it had ever seemed before. He punished her, he loved her, he possessed her.

He dragged his cock all the way out until the head rested against her entrance. Then he'd ram forward again, opening her and stretching her to meet his demands. Over and over again, he repeated the action until she went limp, too exhausted to do more than lie there as he took his pleasure.

Then he slowed as if to prevent his own release. He wasn't as desperate as before and instead he set a steady rhythm destined to keep him just on the brink, hovering as she'd hovered for so long.

"I want another," he growled. "Come for me again, Callie. I won't release you until you do."

His words stirred her to life when she didn't believe she had any left. Her muscles warmed and fluttered and desire coiled deep within and fanned out as flames licked higher.

Each thrust jerked her body, and her cheek rubbed abrasively against the cushion of the couch.

"Come, Callie. Let go. I'll fuck you all night if I have to."

Oh God.

She trembled. Her legs shook, both from the force of his thrusts and her own shattered senses. This time her orgasm rose sharp and fast, so edgy that she feared losing consciousness.

And still he pushed, fucking her with ruthless discipline she wouldn't have imagined any man having. How could he have so much control over his body?

For several minutes he thrust, his hands holding her in a painful grip. Then his hands left her and red-hot pain slashed across her ass as he smacked her.

Her vision dimmed as she finally, finally edged over. Over and over his hand fell as his cock punished her ass, thrusting deep, opening her wider and wider with every push.

She screamed again. Cried out his name in fear. What was happening to her frightened her. Not him. Her own body. Her own complete loss of control. She fought desperately to maintain consciousness but darkness was quickly closing around her.

Her release flashed like a violent thunderstorm, so vicious, so wonderfully pleasurable, like nothing she'd ever experienced in her life. How could he do this to her? How could he unlock such a primitive response?

On the hazy edge of her consciousness she was aware of him pulling from her clenching pussy. Hot liquid spurted onto her back, onto her ass, inside her ass. Down her legs.

Then he slid back inside her ass, forcing his semen deeper into her body. For a long moment he simply slid back and forth, his entry eased by the slick liquid.

He came to a stop and held himself deep. She could feel him soften some from the turgid hardness of just a moment ago.

She closed her eyes, unwilling to continue the battle to remain conscious. Max was there. Max would take care of her.

Chapter Twenty-One

Max carefully pushed himself off Callie and pulled from her quivering body. He stared down at the beautiful woman who'd given herself unreservedly. She taken everything he had to give and asked—no demanded—more.

Love filled his chest, swelled in his throat until he was incapable of speech. Something inside him cracked open at the sight of her lying there, eyes closed, exhausted from all she'd endured.

Tenderness flooded into his heart. He walked around to the side of the couch and gathered her gently into his arms. He lifted her up and carried her toward the bedroom. He set her on the bed only long enough for him to hurry into the bathroom and start the water.

He made it hot, and soon steam rose as the water tumbled out of the faucet. Leaving it, he returned to the bedroom to find Callie curled on her side, her eyes still closed.

"My *dolcezza*," he murmured as he kissed her temple.

He smoothed her hair away from her face and then gathered her in his arms once more. He carried her into the bathroom and murmured her name until her eyelids fluttered open and her cloudy blue eyes stared back at him, warm with love and contentment.

"I've drawn a bath for you. I want you to enjoy a nice long

soak."

"Mmm. That sounds nice."

He lowered her into the water, and she let out a blissful sigh. As soon as she was submerged up to her shoulders, she leaned her head back and fixed her sleepy gaze on him.

He palmed the top of her head and then rubbed his hand down to her nape. "Are you all right? Was I too rough with you?"

Her smile was dazzling. It took his breath away. It was like being punched in the stomach. So much love and...trust. Finally, trust.

"You were wonderful, Max. I've never felt anything like it. I'm not even sure I have words to describe it."

He leaned down and pressed his lips to her forehead. For a long moment, he remained there, eyes closed as he simply savored her sweetness.

"Soak, my love. I want you well taken care of. I'm going to go prepare a snack and some wine. I'll bring it in for you to have in your bath. Call me if the water cools. I'll draw more hot."

Again she gifted him with a sweet smile that tightened his gut all over again. He didn't want to leave her. Even for as long as it would take to get her something to eat and drink.

Reluctantly he left the bathroom and went into the kitchen to make sandwiches. He cut a selection of cheeses and prepared a small fruit bowl. He'd made certain his apartment was stocked with her favorite wine, and he pulled a bottle out along with two glasses.

He arranged everything on a tray and walked back into the bathroom where Callie was dozing in the tub. He quietly set the tray down and then leaned over to run his fingers through the water.

It was warm but not hot, so he turned the faucet back on, and Callie came awake, her eyes startled and confused.

"Sorry. The water's growing cold. I don't want you to get a chill."

She smiled. "Thank you, Max."

When he was satisfied with the temperature of the water, he handed her a glass of wine and then took the platter in hand and perched on the edge of the tub.

Tenderly he offered her a bite of sandwich and then followed it with a small hunk of cheese. After she took a sip of wine, he slid a grape between her lips and listened to her low hum of appreciation as the sweet fruit burst onto her tongue.

He was content to see to her needs. He wanted her well rested and satisfied. He wanted her to feel safe and provided for. Like she was the only woman in the world who mattered to him.

She sipped lazily at the wine and yawned before shaking her head when he offered another piece of fruit.

"Had enough?"

"Yes, thank you. I feel so unbelievably spoiled right now."

He smiled and stroked his hand over her cheek. "That's precisely how I want you to feel. Always. Cherished and pampered beyond measure."

She sighed and leaned back, closing her eyes as she rested her head against the rim.

"Tired?"

"Mmm-hmm."

"If you'll finish your bath, I'll dry you off and we'll go to bed."

Her eyes popped open. "Only if you're ready. It's early yet."

Her worry brought another smile to his face. "I can see you're tired, *dolcezza*. I have no wish to exhaust you. I can think of nothing better than to go to bed and have you wrap your sweet body around mine."

He stroked his finger down her arm and lingered over the silver cuff at her wrist. Seeing his brands of possession at her wrists fired a raw, primitive instinct deep within his soul.

No modern man should feel this possessive of a woman. And yet he did. He couldn't muster one iota of regret for it either.

She was his. Utterly and completely his.

He looked up to see her also looking at the jewelry on her wrists. He continued to stroke one finger over the cool metal.

"Do you like them?"

"I love them," she said huskily. "The sentiment is beautiful, Max. I swear you have a poet's soul."

The obvious appreciation in her voice warmed him through. He loved showering her with things. Anything to make her happy, to make her look at him like he held the world in his hands.

He had so many plans for them. He wanted to take her places she hadn't yet been. He wanted to experience the joy in her eyes when she saw the sunset in a new part of the world.

They were truly two halves of a whole. Two drifters. Restless. Free-spirited. Never content with the same routine.

"What are you thinking?"

He blinked and realized she was staring thoughtfully at him. Then he smiled. "I was imagining taking you places you've never been and watching the sunsets together."

Her eyes instantly glowed and her smile was so radiant it lit up the entire room. "There's no one I'd rather be with than you,

Max."

"It's a damn good thing," he growled playfully.

She laughed and reached for the soap at the end of the tub. "Give me a few minutes to wash and then I'll get out and you can haul me to bed. I'm not entirely certain I can walk."

"I'll go turn back the sheets, and then I'll be back with a towel. Take your time, *dolcezza*. There's no hurry tonight."

Callie watched him go and then heaved a huge sigh of contentment. Her body ached. No doubt about it. Muscles she didn't even know she had were sore. Her bottom throbbed. She was so tired she was about to fall over, but she'd never felt more happy and alive in her life.

She scrubbed soap over her body, rising up from the water to get all the girl parts and then quickly sinking down into the hot water when chill bumps danced their way across her skin.

When Max returned with a huge, plush towel, she was eager to get dried off and warm again. She stepped from the tub and into the towel he promptly wrapped around her, his arms going around her as well.

For a long moment he hugged her tight as the towel soaked up all the moisture. Then he carefully rubbed over her skin, making sure to dry every inch. By the time he finished, cold was the last thing she felt.

She was heated from the inside out. Flushed. Flames stoked. Even as her knees trembled with fatigue, she yearned for Max. Wanted his touch. His kiss. His possession all over again.

When she was dry, he tucked his arm underneath her legs and lifted her into his arms as he strode toward the bedroom. The covers were turned back, and he slid her onto the mattress before promptly pulling the covers up to her shoulders.

He puttered around for a moment, undressing and turning off the bathroom lights. He left the lamp on his side burning and then climbed into bed beside her.

As soon as he lay down, she snuggled into his arms. He held her and stroked his palms up and down her sides, over her curves, her hips, her breasts, like he couldn't get enough of touching her.

She nuzzled into his neck and kissed him just below the ear. "Love you."

"Love you too, *dolcezza.*"

"There's so much I want to share with you," she said wistfully.

He pulled away and stared curiously at her. "Like what?"

"My home. The mountain. All the places that are so special to me. As much of a roamer as I am, my heart will always be on that mountain. It's a place I can always return to and know that I'm loved and accepted no matter what."

"I can't wait for you to share it with me. I'm looking forward to seeing the things you most cherish."

"I'll take you to Callie's Meadow. It's where I was born."

He went still against her and his hand stopped its progress over the swell of her hip. "It sounds like a beautiful place."

"Oh it is," she breathed. "It's always been special to the family because it's where my mom gave birth to me. But over the years it somehow became mine. My refuge. My dream place. One day I'm going to build my own house there. I've designed it in my head so many times that it's become real."

"And where do I fit in to this dream?"

She pushed up on her elbow, her hair falling over her breasts as she stared earnestly down at him. "Where do you want to fit in, Max? I'm winging it here. I have no idea what your plans are. You say you love me. I love you. For most people that means they're going to try to have a relationship. A serious relationship. But we've not talked about it at all. I have no idea what you have in mind."

"You're mine," he said simply. "What that means is that you're going to be with me. Whether it means a lifelong commitment or marriage on paper. I don't care. Those things aren't as important as your promise to belong to me, to submit to me, to accept our relationship and to wear the brands of my possession."

"But what does that mean?" she asked softly.

Her heart was thumping so hard, she feared it would beat right out of her chest. She hated moments like this. She wasn't versed in being all subtle and coy. She was too blunt. Too demanding. Too damn honest for her own good.

"Where will we live? I assume you want us to be together. I don't want to leave my life, my family. They're too important to me. So tell me, Max. What does that mean for us?"

He hushed her with a kiss, and for several long seconds, neither of them spoke as he kissed her over and over until she nearly forgot what she'd asked.

"It means you're mine and I'm not letting you go. It means that your happiness is the most important thing in my life. I've promised to take care of you. To place your needs above mine. To cherish your gift of submission. That doesn't mean that I'll fly in on weekends so we can have a quick fuck before we go our separate ways. It means you're going to spend every goddamn day in my arms, in my bed, underneath me, me inside you as many times as I can get there."

She could barely breathe for the hope burning like a torch in her soul.

"We'll stay on your damn mountain if that's what you want,

Callie. I'm not going to take you away from the place and the people you love."

"Oh Max."

She threw her arms around him, nearly sending him rolling from the bed in her exuberance. She landed atop him, arms and legs sprawled as she peppered him with kisses.

He laughed and tried to ward her off but she persisted until he put his hands up and begged for mercy.

"Lord but you get crazy when you're happy, Callie."

She grinned, straddled him and stared down as her hands gripped his shoulders. "You make me happy. I don't think it's possible to be happier than I am right now."

"I sincerely hope you're wrong," he said softly. "For me, I can only imagine how happy we'll be on our wedding day. On the day you give birth to our first child. Our fourth child. Or our fifth. Or maybe when you look at me in fifty years like you're looking at me right now."

"You have to stop," she choked out. "You're going to make me cry again."

He reached for her and pulled her down into his arms. "We can't have that. I don't like it when you cry. It makes me feel helpless, and I hate feeling helpless."

"Let's go home tomorrow," she urged. "I know you wanted us to spend a week here, but we have all the time in the world. I want you to meet my family. I want you to see all the things I love."

He hesitated a moment as he ran his hand over her hair. Then his chest heaved as he sighed. "All right. We'll go back tomorrow. If we're going to build our future, it's important that I meet your family and see the things that are precious to you."

Callie wrapped her arms around him and hugged him

close. "You'll like my family. They can be overbearing, but they love me and I love them."

"Anyone who loves you as much as I do can't be all bad," he said.

She raised her head to see his grin, and she smiled back as sunshine poured over her soul. Perfect. Things were just perfect. They couldn't be any more so.

She wanted to bounce out of bed and call her mother as she'd almost done in Europe when she'd first met Max. She wanted to tell her that she had indeed met the man she was going to marry.

But she was too comfortable wrapped around Max like a blanket, and she yawned broadly as she snuggled more firmly into his embrace. The call to her mom could wait until tomorrow.

Chapter Twenty-Two

"I'm thinking we should ditch your car when we get to Clyde and take my truck up the mountain," Callie said as they passed the sign that signaled three more miles until they reached their destination.

Max's mouth turned down into a grimace. "Your truck is on its last leg, Callie. I hate that you still drive it. It's an accident waiting to happen."

She rolled her eyes. "You sound just like my dads. And my brothers. They've been nagging me forever to get something else. My dads are dying to buy me a new vehicle."

"You won't let them?"

His expression suggested she was nuts, and yeah, her truck was old. It had definitely seen better days. The idea of riding in such a thing probably appalled Max. His tastes ran to the more refined. And expensive.

"I can't afford one," she said.

When he continued to look at her with a blank expression she sighed.

"I've never allowed my parents to just buy stuff for me. They have money. But it's not *my* money. Everything I've earned I've stashed away for my dream house. As long as my truck runs, then it's money I don't have to invest into a new car and

I'm closer to my dream of my own place."

He frowned. "You're still thinking like someone who's not in a relationship."

"Until a few days ago I wasn't," she said lightly. "It's hard to adjust a lifetime's worth of thinking in a few days. You have to be patient with me, Max. I'm used to being independent. I've always gone my own way. My dream of building my house won't go away just because you and I are together. It's something I'll continue to work for."

His frown deepened and his fingers curled tighter around the steering wheel. "Do you honestly think I'll allow you to continue working menial jobs—in a bar, for God's sake—to fund your house?"

Her eyes narrowed, but he held up his hand before she could speak.

"It's not a matter of your submissiveness or my desire to control you, Callie. I hope to hell you never think I'm some controlling bastard who regulates every second of your life. This has nothing to do with control. I'm concerned for your safety. You can't tell me that working in your brother's bar is something you want to do long-term. Or these other jobs you pick up for extra money. I've got more money than I'll ever use in a lifetime. More than our children will use in their lifetime. Do you honestly expect me to stand by and not give you the money to build your house?"

She sighed and rubbed her head tiredly. It was an argument she'd had many times with her parents. No one seemed to understand how her mind worked. They wanted to take care of her. Buy things for her. Make her life easier. She loved them for it. She truly did. But she wanted her own life. Wanted to be able to look at the things she had and feel a sense of accomplishment.

Her brothers had all forged their own path independent of their parents. Seth was a cop—a damn good cop. Michael was a veterinarian with a thriving practice. And Dillon... Dillon had a Midas touch when it came to business. He probably owned half of Clyde. His bar would be self-supporting enough, but the bar was a drop in the bucket compared to the other properties and businesses Dillon owned.

And then there was Callie. Callie who didn't have the discipline for college. Who was too antsy and couldn't stay in one place long enough to study for an actual career. Head-in-the-clouds, dreamer Callie.

Her family loved her but Callie knew she was an enigma to them. Someone they adored but never truly understood. The dads probably took turns blaming each other for fathering her. They were all steady and hardworking. How could Callie have popped from their gene pool?

She sighed again as she saw Max was still watching her, waiting for a response.

"I don't expect you to understand. But I hope you'll accept it—me."

He reached over and took her hand, pulling it to his lips. He kissed each knuckle and then lowered her hand to his lap where he laced his fingers with hers.

"There's nothing about you I don't love and accept, Callie. That doesn't mean I'm not going to fight you on certain matters. There's no way I'm ever going to be okay with you working ridiculously low-paying, dangerous jobs when I have the means to support you, spoil you and take care of you. That's who I am. I don't expect you to understand, but I hope you'll accept it."

She winced. How neatly he turned her words back on her. She couldn't even argue, which irritated her all the more. She glared at him and he merely shot her a smug grin. Yeah, he knew he'd won this round. Damn the man. She usually found his arrogance attractive, but today, she found it...annoying.

Excitement replaced her annoyance as soon as they turned onto Main Street in Clyde. No matter where she went or how long she was gone, when she came home she was filled with happiness.

Max turned into the parking lot of the motel where he'd last stayed and parked beside her SUV. She could tell it pained him to ride in her truck, but she didn't want him taking his car up the mountain.

She grinned and bounced out, opening the door to her truck. She slid into the driver's seat, sighing as the worn leather cupped her behind like a lover. Yeah, she was old, but she was still a good truck and Callie loved her.

Max climbed into the passenger side with a look of exasperation but remained silent as she began backing out of her spot.

Normally she would stop and see Lily or stop in at Michael's practice or even stick her head in at the sheriff's office to say hello to Seth, but she was anxious to go up to her parents' so she could show Max her meadow.

There would be plenty of time to visit with the family later.

Knowing that if she did her usual routine of parking at her parents' house and walking down to the meadow she and Max would get held up by her mom and dads, Callie opted instead to pull off onto the old logging road that would take them to the meadow without going all the way up to her parents'.

She cast a sideways glance at Max. He looked tense. His jaw was set into a tight line and his gaze was sharply taking in their surroundings. The closer they got to the meadow, the darker his expression got.

"Something wrong?"

He shook his head but remained quiet.

With a shrug, she drove around the last bend and then parked in front of the old fence that used to separate Colter land from the meadow.

"This is it," she said with a note of reverence she never seemed to rid herself of when she spoke of her meadow.

Max slowly opened his door and got out. She climbed out and met him around the front of her truck.

"Why the fence?" he asked. "I thought your family owned all of the property up here."

She frowned a moment. She didn't remember going into detail, but then Max knew her parents owned a lot of land so it was a natural assumption.

She slid her hand into Max's and urged him toward the worn, wooden fence.

"We just never took this part down. Someday I'll get to it. It was up when the previous people owned the meadow. My dads tried to buy it for years with no success. Then when my mom got pregnant with me, they suddenly wanted to sell. My dads bought it as a surprise for my mom. And, well, you know the rest."

His lips formed a thin line. "Yeah."

"Isn't it beautiful?"

Callie sighed as she stared over the rolling slope of the land to where the creek ran down the middle. Flowers covered the earth in a blanket of vivid color that took her breath away.

"It's the most beautiful place I've ever seen."

She beamed at Max. "I think so too. Now can you see why I want to build my dream house here?"

He nodded, but he still looked...dark. Thoughtful. She couldn't imagine what was going through his head. Did he think that he somehow took a backseat to her dreams?

She slid her arms around his waist and hugged him, though whether she did so to reassure herself or him she wasn't sure.

"Right over there is where I was born," she said softly as she pointed to the right of the creek and back, closer to where the property adjoined her parents' to the south.

Max smiled. "I imagine you were always an impatient child. Even from the very beginning. Trust you to be born here."

She grinned. "It was perfect. Do you know that of the four of us, only one was born in an actual hospital? We swear that Dillon was switched at birth with one of the other babies. No one could ever figure out where he came from."

"I just hope you don't have any crazy ideas of giving birth in the middle of nowhere," he said with a scowl.

She laughed and squeezed him again. "Oh no. I'm afraid I'm too fond of modern technology. And pain relief! I want to be surrounded by nurses and doctors and the guy giving the epidural."

He kissed her brow and his expression eased. "That's good because I want only the best for you and our child when the time comes."

Her entire heart squeezed ridiculously until she felt near to exploding. How could she possibly be this happy when just days ago she'd been miserable? She wanted to pinch herself, but if this was a dream, she was so not ready to wake up yet.

"Come on," she said, pulling at his hand. "Let's go walk down to the stream. I'll pick some flowers for Lily. She loves flowers. She's an artist, you know. She once drew me a picture of the meadow and gave it to me. It's so awesome."

Max smiled as she dragged him to the fence. "You love this

place, don't you, Callie?"

She stopped with one leg slung over the wooden slats. "It's my most favorite place in the world."

There was a hint of sadness in his eyes as he stared back at her. But then he blinked and it was gone. He put his hand out to stop her progress and then he hopped the fence with ease. He reached back and hoisted her over, then laced his fingers with hers once more.

"Let's go see your meadow, *dolcezza*. I'm happy to spend as much time here as you like."

She went up on tiptoe to kiss him. "Thank you, Max. I love you so much."

He caught her chin and turned her toward his mouth. "And I love you."

She smiled as she pulled away and then she dropped his hand and took off at a run. "Come on!" she called over her shoulder. "Last one there gets a spanking."

Max's laughter followed her as she ran full tilt down the hill toward the bubbling creek. She knew he'd catch her—which was the point. Max was an adventurous guy, but no way he'd allow her to spank him.

He caught her just a few feet from the stream. He likely lagged behind just to give her false hope. He smacked her on the ass and then sped by, reaching the stream a mere three feet in front of her.

She stopped and bent, sucking in deep breaths. Damn the man, he didn't even look winded and she was on the verge of puking.

"You did that on purpose," she accused.

"What?" he asked innocently.

"Waited until the last minute to catch me."

He grinned. "You don't seriously think I'm going to pass on any opportunity to spank that pretty ass of yours, do you?"

"You wouldn't be laughing if you'd screwed up and I beat you."

He chuckled again. "If anyone could ever get away with spanking me, *dolcezza*, it would be you. But no. I'll be the only one dishing out spankings in this relationship."

She turned her lip down into a pout, knowing it would delight him.

He pulled her to him and nibbled at her bottom lip as she knew he would.

"I can guarantee you'll enjoy the spankings every bit as much as I will."

Chapter Twenty-Three

"I can't believe we're staying here again," Max said as he dropped their bags on the floor of the same motel room where he'd spent so many days.

"Shhh," Callie said, shushing him with her hand. "I'm calling Mom."

Max shut the door with a sigh, trudged over to the bed and plopped down on the edge. Then with a dramatic flair he fell back, arms outstretched, and closed his eyes.

Callie laughed and put the phone back to her ear. "Hey Mom!"

"Callie! Where are you? I've been so worried. I can't say it's not like you to run off at a moment's notice, but you have to admit, the circumstances were different this time."

"I'm fine, Mom. Promise. I wanted to let you know that Max and I are back in town. I was hoping to bring him up to meet you soon."

"Of course. We can't wait to meet him, sweetie. When did you want to come up? Where are you staying? You know there's plenty of room here."

"Uhh." Not that she minded being at her parents', but no way did she want her and Max staying there. It would put a serious crimp in their sex life. "Anytime is good for us. The sooner the better. And we're fine. Really. Max has a room at the motel."

"Oh Callie. That motel is horrible."

"We're good, Mom. Now when do you want us up?"

"Tomorrow. Definitely tomorrow. I'll have your dads fix a nice dinner. No, maybe lunch is better. Let's plan on lunch and then we can spend the afternoon getting to know Max."

"That sounds great. We'll come up around eleven."

"Terrific. We'll see you then."

"Thanks, Mom."

"Callie?"

Callie put the phone back to her ear. "Yes?"

"Are you happy?"

Callie smiled until her teeth ached. "Yeah, Mom. I'm happier than I ever imagined."

"That's all I care about, then."

"I love you, Mom."

"Love you too, baby. See you tomorrow."

Callie hung up and turned to see Max watching her from the bed.

"They want us up for lunch tomorrow. The entire family will be there. I have no doubt my mom is even now on the phone rounding up the rest of her brood and issuing orders to be there or die."

Max chuckled. "She sounds like a tyrant. I wonder where on earth you got your personality from."

Callie flopped down beside him and hit him with a pillow. "My mom is the sweetest person on earth, but yes, she still rules the roost with a velvet fist."

Max wrapped his arms around her and then pulled her

across his lap before she had time to respond. His hand settled on her jeans-covered ass and his laughter sounded wicked in her ear.

"Now, it seems I owe you a spanking."

She went limp and white-hot desire sizzled through her body, prickling her skin. It amazed her how instantly aware she became around this man. A word. A touch. Just a look and she was putty in his hands.

"Better make sure I don't scream," she muttered. "My brother's the sheriff, remember? Last thing I want is him breaking down our door because someone reported that I was being murdered in a hotel room."

Max rubbed his hand over her behind. "Oh you'll enjoy this one, *dolcezza*. I know I plan to."

Callie was a nervous wreck. Why, she didn't know. This was only one of the most important days of her entire life. Her family, who meant the world to her, was going to meet and stand in judgment of the man she loved more than anything.

Yeah, good reason to be nervous.

If only she hadn't poured out her hurt to her family. If she'd only waited...they wouldn't be coming into the meeting with Max with prejudice.

She sighed. Woe be unto the man who hurt her dads' little girl. Her brothers weren't much better. They'd probably all glower at Max the entire time.

"Quit biting your lip, *dolcezza*. You're going to ruin that pretty mouth of yours."

She glanced over to see Max studying her. He'd insisted on taking his car to her parents', and she hadn't argued. She wanted Max to feel comfortable and on equal footing.

"I'm just…nervous."

"Yes, I can see that. You need to stop worrying so much. Your parents will see how madly in love I am with you. Isn't that what every parent wants for their child? Someone to love them and take care of them?"

It was on the tip of her tongue to tell him that her family knew everything, but that would only make Max uptight and there was no sense in them both being on edge. Besides, Max probably knew. He knew how close she was to her family, and she and Max had been apart for several months. Who wouldn't have come home and told their family what a scumbag he was?

By the time they pulled into her parents' drive, Callie's stomach was in knots. She rubbed her damp palms down the legs of her pants as Max parked beside her mom's SUV.

She didn't have long to contemplate whether she wanted to get out because her mom appeared on the porch, a wide smile on her face. Before Callie had her door opened, Holly Colter was down the steps and hurrying toward the vehicle.

Thank goodness for Max. He was out with a warm smile and hand outstretched while Callie still hung halfway out of the car.

"Hello, Mrs. Colter. I'm Max. It's nice to finally meet you."

Callie stumbled out as her mom enfolded Max in a warm hug.

"Hello, Max. And please, do call me Holly. It's wonderful to meet you too."

"Hi Mom."

Holly turned to Callie and just as quickly pulled her into a bone-crushing hug.

"Mom," Callie said with a laugh. "You just saw me a few

days ago."

Holly pulled back with a muttered *hmph.* "I don't care if it's only been a few hours. I'm entitled to be happy to see you. I have to make up for all the time you spend from home."

Callie hugged her again and all her unease melted away in her mother's embrace.

Holly pulled back and then grabbed at Callie's and Max's hands. "Come on inside, you two. Your dads are waiting to meet Max, Callie."

Callie smiled over at Max who wore an expression that looked like a cross of awe and confusion. Holly dragged them both toward the door and all but shoved them through.

Ethan stood in the living room. Though he opened his arms for Callie, he looked at Max with an indecipherable expression on his face.

"Be good," Callie whispered as she hugged her dad.

Ethan kissed her cheek and then extended his hand to Max. "I'm Ethan Colter, one of Callie's dads."

"Max Wilder," Max said as he shook Ethan's hand.

One down, two to go.

"Where are the other dads?" Callie asked.

"In the kitchen. You and Max get comfortable. I'll go get them," Holly said.

Callie perched on the couch next to Max and laced her fingers through his.

"Isn't it me who should be nervous?" Max murmured. "Relax, Callie. I'm pretty sure they won't threaten to kick *your* ass."

Callie burst into laughter, which caused Ethan to raise an eyebrow in their direction.

Just then Holly returned with Adam and Ryan in tow. Predictably, both dads' faces were set in stone. Callie rose and when their gazes alighted on her, they softened and warmth entered their eyes.

She hugged Adam first and then went into Ryan's arms. He squeezed her tight and then pulled her to his side as both dads stared Max down.

"Stop," Callie hissed. "Give him a chance."

With a grunt, Ryan disentangled himself from Callie and closed the distance between him and Max. He stuck out his hand. "Ryan Colter. Glad to meet you."

Max shook his hand and then extended it in Adam's direction. "Glad to meet you, sir."

"Where is everyone else?" Callie asked, breaking the silence. "Are they coming?"

Holly nodded. "They're on their way. Why don't you come help me in the kitchen a moment, Callie?"

Callie's mouth popped open. Ethan tried hard to suppress a smile but failed miserably. Holly frowned at them both and then tucked Callie's hand into her own and pulled her toward the kitchen.

"So, Max, tell us about yourself," Ryan said.

Holly shoved Callie into the kitchen so she heard no more.

"Subtle, Mom. Real subtle."

Holly scowled at her daughter. "Better to let your dads interrogate Max without you in the room. Let them do their male bonding or beating their chest or whatever it is they do and we'll sit in here and have a glass of tea."

"Poor Max," Callie sighed.

"He looks quite able to handle anything your fathers throw at him."

"Soooo, what do you think?" Callie asked.

Holly plunked down on a barstool and her eyes sparkled as she looked back at Callie. "He's gorgeous, Callie! And the way he looks at you. There's no doubt he cares a lot about you."

"He loves me," Callie said softly. "And I love him."

"So you've worked things out?"

Callie nodded. "Yeah. We're getting there."

Holly reached for her wrists and turned them over as she stared at the silver bands. "What are these? They're beautiful. So feminine and delicate looking!"

Callie's cheeks warmed. How could she possibly explain their significance to her mother?

"Max bought them for me," she said in a low voice.

Holly leaned closer and peered at the engraving. "Oh, that's lovely. Such a wonderful sentiment. That's funny. He doesn't strike me as an expressive sort of man."

Callie smiled. "Oh? What does he strike you as?"

Holly frowned for a moment, her lips pursed in thought. "He seems...hard. Unyielding. Like someone used to getting his way, which of course would never work with you so clearly I'm wrong. You're such a hardhead. Always have gone your own way, much to your fathers' and my despair."

Laughter bubbled out, nearly choking Callie. If her mother only knew.

"You're pretty dead-on," Callie said. "Max is very used to getting his own way."

"Until he met you, anyway," Holly said cheekily.

She wouldn't blush. She would not give herself away. She bit her cheek and remained silent, content to let her mom make of her relationship what she wanted. What was between her and Max was private. She wasn't comfortable with her family knowing the dynamics of their relationship. It would only cause them concern, because they'd never imagine her happy in a situation where she gave up so much control.

"Oh look, the guys are here with Lily," Holly said as she craned her neck to look out the kitchen window.

Eager to see her sister-in-law, Callie hurried from the kitchen. She cast a quick glance to see her fathers deep in conversation with Max. No one looked like they were ready to kill anyone else, so she took that as a good sign.

Dillon was first inside. He hugged Callie fiercely and cast a dark look in Max's direction. He moved to the side to hug his mom but made no effort to walk over to Max.

Lily was next inside and Callie pounced on her immediately. Lily hugged her and then whispered urgently in Callie's ear. "There's something I have to tell you."

Callie pulled away in puzzlement. "What's wrong?"

Lily's mouth turned down into an unhappy frown. "It's Seth. He's been doing some checking."

Lily was cut off when Seth barreled through the door, his face grimmer than Callie had ever seen it. It went beyond his sheriff look when he tried to be all intimidating. He looked...pissed.

"Seth, what on earth is going on?" Callie asked.

Seth paused, his gaze softening. He pulled Callie into his arms. "I'm sorry for what I'm about to tell you, baby girl."

"Seth Colter, what's the meaning of this?" Holly demanded, hands on hips in true don't-mess-with-mama mode.

Callie's fathers rose from their seats, answering frowns on their faces as Michael trailed in behind Seth not looking any happier than his two brothers.

Panic scuttled around Callie's belly until she felt near to

puking. What was going on? Why were they so angry? Why were they all looking at Max like they wanted to murder him?

She instinctively moved away from her brothers and to Max. He was there, putting his arm around her and pulling her into his side. Seth's nostrils flared as he stared angrily at Max.

"I'm going to kill you for what you've done, you son of a bitch."

Chapter Twenty-Four

"Seth!" Callie gasped.

Seth ignored Callie and advanced on Max. Max pushed Callie toward her father as he faced Seth down. He made no effort to defend himself or even to question what the hell Seth was talking about.

"Whatever you have to say to me can be said outside," Max said. "I don't want Callie involved or hurt."

Seth's lip curled. "She needs to hear what I have to say. You may not want her to hear it, but she needs to know what a bastard you are."

Callie turned toward Max. "Max?"

Max put his hand up. "Let me handle this, *dolcezza*."

"You used her," Seth spit out.

Adam stepped forward, his face drawn into a storm cloud. "Seth, what the hell are you insinuating here? This isn't the time or the place. Not in front of your mother, your sister and your wife."

Callie looked around in bewilderment. Everyone was either angry or confused. Her fathers circled her and Max while her brothers stood in front of them, boring holes in Max.

Michael stepped forward. "Let him talk, Dad. This is important, and Callie needs to hear it, however painful it might be."

Lily stepped up beside Callie and pulled her away from Max before wrapping a supportive arm around her.

"Lily, what's going on?" Callie whispered as her heart squeezed painfully in her chest.

Suddenly her mother was on her other side as if she knew that Callie would need her support more now than at any other time. Callie hated the sympathy that shone in Dillon's and Michael's eyes. Hated the anger that bristled from Seth in black waves.

But most of all she hated the fatalistic look of inevitability in Max's eyes, as if he'd expected this and was resigned to the outcome.

"What is going on?" Callie demanded. "This is *ridiculous*!"

Dillon and Michael flanked Lily and their mom who hugged Callie tight against them. Callie swallowed as she waited. Waited in agony, not knowing what to do, who to listen to. She wanted to go to Max. She wanted to scream at Seth to stop. But the look on Max's face stopped her. There was something terrible in his eyes. The knowledge of his fate. And hers.

Never taking his gaze off Max, Seth began in a terse, clipped voice. "I did some checking on Wilder here. Turns out he has some very interesting connections. He owns Capitol Investment Properties."

Adam sucked in his breath. "I know the name. They've approached me numerous times about selling Callie's Meadow."

Callie looked at her dad and then at Seth in confusion. "So?"

"There's more, Callie," Dillon said in a low voice. "Listen to him."

"Max's mother is the one who sold Callie's Meadow to the

dads," Seth continued.

"Don't you mean she was coerced to sell," Max bit out.

Ryan's head whipped around in surprise. "Coerced? There was no coercion. We'd tried to buy the land many times and the owner always refused."

"My stepfather," Max said. "And no, he wouldn't sell. The property had been in our family for a century. It was a legacy passed down for generation after generation. A legacy that should have been mine and my sister's."

Callie went numb. Her blood turned to ice and she simply stared at Max, too baffled to comprehend what was happening. But the anger and bitterness in Max's voice came through loud and clear. It was unmistakable.

"After your...stepfather...passed away, your mother came to me," Adam said tersely. "I'd already given up trying to get your stepfather to sell. She said she needed the money, and believe me, I paid more than the land was worth because we wanted it that much. She said she had two children to raise and that her husband had left her in poor circumstances."

"Bullshit," Max swore.

"The fact is, he came after you, Callie," Seth interjected. "He tracked you, he seduced you for a reason. He wanted your land. The coincidence of the two of you meeting in Europe and falling into a relationship is staggering. After the dads turned his company down the last time, suddenly he shows up in Europe and meets you?"

Something inside Callie crumbled. She looked at Max, begging him to deny the charge. What she saw stunned her. She saw guilt. Regret. Worry. And anger.

She stepped forward. "Tell me it isn't true. Tell me you didn't do what he said you did."

Max looked at her with death in his eyes. "It was true then. It's not true now."

Her stomach revolted. Pain crashed through her chest until she could barely breathe. How stupid was she? Once hadn't been enough. She'd been gullible a second time. She'd made it so easy for Max. He'd torn her apart once already. And she'd let him back in with a whispered apology and words of love. Now her entire family was gathered to witness her shame. Her utter humiliation.

She took another step forward, her legs shaking so badly that it was a miracle she remained standing.

"You lied to me. You manipulated me. You abused your control over me. What were you going to do, Max, use my submission to get your way? Would you have commanded me to sign over my land? Or maybe when we got married you were going to take over everything. Little submissive Callie would never tell you no, right?"

"That's a rotten thing to say," Max snarled. "What we have is real, Callie. I'd never use my dominance to manipulate you."

Behind her, the dads cursed. Her brothers stepped forward, but she held up her hand. There was nothing left for her to lose at this point. No secret left covered. Every little dirty detail of her life had been exposed. She'd never felt more betrayed in her life.

"Tell me you didn't do this," she said tearfully. "Tell me you didn't set up our meeting in Europe. Tell me it was all one huge coincidence."

"I can't tell you that, *dolcezza.* I won't lie to you. I did engineer the meeting. What I didn't engineer was what happened afterward. The way I fell for you."

"Oh God, stop. Just stop it."

Tears spilled down her cheeks as her entire world shattered

into tiny pieces and lay on the floor like jagged shards of glass.

Max moved swiftly to her and grasped her shoulders as he stared intently into her eyes. “Don’t do this, Callie. Listen to me. I *love* you.”

“Can you look me in the eye and tell me you never hoped to coerce me into giving you Callie’s Meadow? Can you do that?”

He was silent for a moment and in his eyes she saw the terrible truth. A sob welled in her throat and swelled outward until she physically couldn’t take a breath. The room blurred in front of her.

Around her, her family erupted into chaos. Her brothers were shouting. Her fathers pressed forward, angry accusations flying as they pushed in between her and Max.

She fell to her knees, her face in her hands as horrible, terrible sounds tore from her throat. Her mother knelt beside her and pulled her into her arms as she rocked back and forth.

But it was too much. Too painful. She couldn’t bear for her family to see her so utterly devastated.

She bolted to her feet and flew toward the door. Max’s anguished cry followed her.

“Callie!”

Covering her ears, she ran for her fathers’ Land Rover, praying the keys were in the ignition as they often were.

Ryan called after her. But she ignored her father and threw herself into the driver’s seat. She had to get away. Away from the pain. Away from Max and his betrayal. Away from the sympathy simmering in her family’s eyes.

She drove recklessly down the drive but when she reached the end, she slowed, determined not to add more stupidity to her list of crimes. She took in steadying breaths and then set off again down the winding switchbacks, no clear direction in mind.

Away. All she knew was that she had to be away.

Tears streamed silently down her cheeks, and then the glint of silver caught her eye and she stared numbly at the cuffs on her wrists.

She braked sharply and then buried her face against the steering wheel as she broke down and allowed the sobs to tear painfully from her chest.

"You were a bastard to do this to her," Max snarled at her brother. "How could you have humiliated her like this? How could you have upset her so badly?"

Seth's mouth gaped open and fury glinted in his eyes. "You're the son of a bitch who used her, Wilder. And don't give me that crap about how it started out that way but changed. You broke her heart once. You dumped her in Europe and then waited months before you came crawling back like a fucking cockroach."

"You should have come to *me*!" Max roared as he jabbed a finger into his own chest. "You should have never hurt her by airing this in front of the people she loves the most. Do you have any idea how lucky you all are? All she ever talks about is how much she adores her family, how important you all are to her, how her dream is to build a home in her meadow so she can be close to you all. And yet you shit on her by dumping this on her without warning. This could have been handled so differently. You could have been man enough to approach me away from her. You could have talked to her privately if you felt you absolutely had to tell her yourself. I could have saved you a hell of a lot of trouble if you'd just come to me. I love that girl. I love her more than my promise to my family. I love her more than the legacy passed on to me by the man who raised me as his son. I love her enough that I was willing to move to this godforsaken town so she'd be happy. I would have done *anything* for her. Anything in the world but hurt her the way you've hurt her."

Max felt like someone had knifed him right in the gut. He broke off from his impassioned speech just as Seth got into his face, his eyes shooting fire.

"The way I've hurt her? I didn't lie to her, you son of a bitch. I've never lied to my sister. I didn't use her. I didn't manipulate her. I want to know what the fuck she's talking about when she talks about your dominance and your control. Just what kind of hold do you have over her?"

"I'd like to know that myself," Ethan spoke up in a deadly quiet voice.

"We all would," Adam said menacingly.

Max swiped his hand over his face. "Fuck this. I'm not explaining my relationship with Callie to you. I don't owe you any explanations. The only person I owe anything to is *her*."

"If you think you're walking out that door, you've lost your mind," Dillon Colter said when Max started past Seth.

"Yeah? Try and stop me."

Chapter Twenty-Five

So it hadn't been the smartest thing to take on six very pissed-off men. Max lay on the bed in his motel room and winced when he tried to move his fist.

For old guys, Callie's fathers could still move fast and they had fists like hammers. Dillon was a freaking mountain by himself and Seth and Michael were lean and muscled and they'd definitely gotten their shots in.

Max hadn't gone down without a fight, though. He'd given as good as he'd gotten and the Colters would be feeling it just as much as he currently was.

He rolled to his side and sucked in his breath when a particularly tender area of his ribs pressed against the mattress. He stared out the window, just as he'd done for the past several hours, waiting for Callie to show up.

She'd at least come for her truck, wouldn't she? She couldn't stay away forever, and when she came, he'd be waiting. He wasn't going to let her go without one hell of a fight. He'd sit on her if he had to.

He'd argue.

He'd fight.

He'd get on his hands and knees and *beg*.

Whatever it took to make her listen. To make her believe he

loved her with everything he had.

He closed his eyes as the memory of her devastation flashed through his mind. She'd looked defeated. And so terribly hurt. He'd never forget that look. He'd live with it for the rest of his life.

"Come back to me, Callie," he whispered. "Give me the chance to make it right."

Callie didn't react to the sound of a truck engine as it neared. She sat in the darkness, her knees drawn to her chest as she stared up into the star-filled sky. The moon cast a pale glow over the meadow and from a distance, the sound of bubbling water reached her ears.

This was her place. Her haven. Her refuge. The one place above all that brought her peace.

Now it was her hell.

An arm curled around her shoulders and she was pulled into a warm embrace.

"I thought I'd find you here," Ryan Colter said.

She turned into his chest and buried her face. "Oh Dad."

It was all she could say. All she had the strength for. She broke off in a sob when she didn't think she had any more tears to shed.

He held her and rocked her back and forth, all the while smoothing a gentle hand over her hair.

"Your mother's frantic. Adam and Ethan are pacing the floors. Your brothers want to mount a lynch party for Max and run him out of town. Seth seriously wants to arrest him for some trumped-up infraction and lock him in jail for several days."

"But you're here," she choked out.

"I'm here."

"How did you know?"

"This is where you've always come when you're hurting, baby girl. From the time you were little this was your place. Remember when you were eight years old and you threatened to run away? You even packed a bag and left the house. Your mama nearly died. Adam about had a heart attack. None of them thought you'd actually do it. Me? I came here because I knew it's where you'd be. It's where you always run to."

She wrapped her arms around his waist and laid her head on his chest as she'd done so many times in her life. Her dads had always been there for her. The ups and downs. Good times and bad. Her family had always been the one constant in her life.

"I hurt so much," she whispered.

He kissed the top of her head. "I know, baby. I know you do. I wish I could take it all away. I wish I could snap my fingers and the pain would disappear."

"I was such an idiot. I feel so...stupid."

"You should never feel stupid for loving someone, Callie girl. You gave him something wonderful, and he shit on it in return. That's on him. Not you. Never you. One day he'll look back and know he gave up the best thing that ever happened to him. He'll have to live with that loss for the rest of his life."

"I loved him so much, Dad. I trusted him. Even after what he did. He said all the right things. It was like he knew me, and I guess he did. He certainly studied up on me enough. I feel like such an idiot. I took him out here. I babbled on about my dream house and how much the land meant to me, and all the while he stood there hating me, resenting me and my family for taking his birthright, and he schemed to get it back."

Her dad went quiet for a long moment. His breath came out in audible huffs as he seemed to struggle with what he wanted to say next.

"Callie, honey, there's something I need to ask you. You said... You said some things to Max that worry me. You talked about control and dominance. Those are two serious matters. I need to know if he ever hurt you."

"No," she said sadly. "Not in the way you mean. He's never physically hurt me. I know you won't understand—"

"Try me," he challenged.

"God," she muttered. "This is so not a conversation I want to have with my dad."

Ryan pulled away and she could see his utter seriousness reflected in the moonlight. "There's nothing you can't talk to me about, Callie. You know that. Now if you'd feel better talking to your mother, I'll be happy to bring you home so you can have this conversation with her, but I'd rather you talk to me about it."

Callie sighed. "I know it might be hard to believe, but I'm submissive. At least with Max. I can't say it's something that's built into me because I've certainly never been submissive in any of my other relationships. Quite the opposite, actually. I probably wore the pants in most of them.

"Max... He's a dominant force. He just exudes this aura of power. When I was with him, I wanted nothing more than to please him, and I won't lie, he took very good care of me. Very, very good care. He saw to my every need. He anticipated my needs," she corrected. "He often knew what I wanted or needed before I did."

Ryan picked up her wrist so that the silver bands gleamed in the moonlight. "And these? Are they a symbol of his ownership?"

Callie was silent for a long time. "Yes," she said quietly. "They are—were."

Ryan sighed. "I can't say I like to hear any of this. You're my little girl—will always be my little girl. You're in a position where power is easily abused. That worries me. It takes a very special man to have that kind of control over a woman and truly love and cherish her."

"Yes, it does," she returned sadly. "I thought Max was one of them."

Ryan hugged her to him again. "I just want you to be careful, honey. We love you so much."

"I love you too, Dad. All of you."

"Your brothers are worried about you. Especially Seth. He's feeling pretty awful about the way he dropped this on you. He was pissed at Max and he was angry at the way he'd used you, and you know Seth. He's intensely protective of those he loves. He doesn't always think before he acts."

"I wish he'd told me privately," Callie admitted. "That was probably the most humiliating experience of my life. But I'm not angry with him. I know he did it because he loves me and wants to protect me."

"Don't feel humiliated, baby. We're your family. We love you and want what's best for you. We were all surprised, and angry. I don't want you to feel self-conscious around us now. That's the last thing we want. We're here for you. Always. This is your home."

"I just want to know if it'll ever stop hurting."

Just the words made her eyes sting and her nose draw up. She closed her eyes as more hot tears slipped down her cheeks.

"I can't answer that, baby girl. We've told you the story about when your mother took it upon herself to protect me and your other dads and she left us for our own good."

He nearly snorted as he got to that part. Callie had indeed heard the story before. It never failed to get her dads riled up, but now she listened to it with new understanding.

"It was the most painful moment of my life. I thought when I was shot and the asshole trying to kill her took her away was the worst moment. Or when I lay in the hospital not knowing if she'd live or die. But the worst was finding her gone from her hospital room and knowing there wasn't a damn thing I could do to bring her back. Your fathers and I had to return home and hope like hell that she would eventually come back to us.

"I don't know if I would have ever stopped hurting. It was the worst few months of my life. But when she walked back through that front door and she was all round and pregnant with Seth, it was the best moment, and the moment only got better after that. Seth's birth. And then Michael and Dillon. And then you.

"We always believed that our family was complete. But not your mother. She was convinced that there was one more Colter yet to be born. You. And when you arrived, I didn't think life could get any better. You completed us, Callie.

"And I said all this to make a point. You hurt like hell now. I know I did when your mother left. But you won't hurt forever. You have a lot of happiness in front of you. Your best times are yet to come."

"I think this is the most I've ever heard you talk at one time," she said, her voice muffled against his chest.

"Smartass," he chided. "I talk when I've got something to say. I have plenty to say when my only daughter is hurting."

"I love you, Dad."

"I love you too, baby girl. Think we could head back so your mama can fuss over her only daughter for a while?"

Callie sighed. The last thing she wanted was to go back to her parents'. But she knew she had to or they'd be worried sick. All she wanted was to be alone and to think. To absorb all that had happened. To rid herself of the sickness that welled up from her soul.

How could she face her family when nothing felt like it would ever be right?

She stared up at the sky again and gazed at the stars that scattered like diamonds. Why did she have to fall so hard for Max? Why had he lied to her? Why make her fall like she had? Why did he have to be so...perfect? But he wasn't. He wasn't real. He was what he wanted her to see. He'd so deftly manipulated her that she'd lost all faith in her ability to read people. How could she trust anyone after this?

Her judgment sucked. She'd even known that she fell back into his arms too quickly, and yet she'd done it anyway. She was partly to blame because she'd been too willing to forgive. But she'd wanted what he'd offered so much that she'd turned a blind eye to the pain he'd already caused her.

As much as she didn't want to go back to her parents', she didn't have a choice because her only other option was to go to Lily's where her brothers would hover and make threats against humanity.

"Callie?"

She drew away and dragged a hand through her bedraggled hair. "Yeah, we can head back. I don't want Mom to worry."

He helped her to her feet and then herded her toward her mom's SUV. "You can ride with me. Your dads and I will come back for the Land Rover later."

Callie nodded because it was far easier to just go along with whatever he wanted. She didn't have the energy to drive anyway.

Chapter Twenty-Six

Callie lay on her bed, staring up at the ceiling, just as she'd done for the last twenty-four hours. Her mom was worried. Her dads were worried. Her brothers had called every hour on the hour.

She didn't have the strength to face their sympathy or their desire to fix things. They couldn't.

She hadn't slept. Oh, she'd wanted to. She could think of nothing better than to escape her reality and just let her mind go blank. Just for a little while. But sleep had eluded her and so she'd lain here, wide-eyed, heart hurting so much and her mind crowded with Max.

The solution was reactionary—let's be honest here—she was running. Just like she'd always done. And as much as she'd like to think she had the will to stand up, face Max and her family, the simple truth was she just wanted to get away from it all.

The more she thought about it, the more the idea took root until it was all she could think about. It helped that it took her mind off the awful, gut-wrenching grief. Action was preferable to lying here with her mom just a few feet away on the other side of that door, silent and worrying.

She sat up and swung her feet over the edge of the bed. When she got up, she bobbled a bit and stood there a moment while she regained her balance. Then she strode to her dresser and looked at herself in the mirror.

She looked awful. No amount of makeup would cover the raw grief etched into her face. She wasn't even going to try.

What she had to do shouldn't take long. She traveled light. Always had. A trip to the bank and then to the realtor's office and she could be on her way to the airport.

She latched on to her plan of action with single-minded pursuit. Now that she had hatched the idea, it simply wouldn't go away and it became what she *had* to do, not what she wanted.

She glanced around, trying to figure out what she should bring, but it took too much energy. There wasn't anything she needed that couldn't be bought later.

Grabbing for her purse, she went to the door and opened it, expecting to see her mom or one of the dads in the hall. Thankfully it was empty.

Blessed numbness gripped her like ice as she walked toward the living room. It was such a relief. No more pain. No more tears. She walked like a robot and performed as such. Her mind had shut off and now she only had one focus.

"Callie!"

She turned slowly, knowing her stare was probably as blank as she felt. Her mother stood in the living room looking pale and worried. Ethan was beside her, his dark eyes stroking gently over Callie, threatening to break the wall of ice.

Holly rushed toward Callie. "Are you all right? Would you like something to eat?"

The lie came easily. Before Max, she'd never lied to her parents. Doing so now should have made her feel awful, but curiously, she felt no regret.

"I'm going to see Lily."

Holly frowned and looked toward Ethan, a silent plea for help.

"If you want to go see Lily, I'll drive you," Ethan said in a soft voice. "You shouldn't drive right now."

Callie shook her head and even mustered a smile. "I'm fine. Really. Can I borrow your truck? Mine's still in town. I'll ask Dillon to make sure you get it back."

Ethan glanced at Holly and then back to Callie. "Baby, you look...awful. I think I should drive you."

She hadn't wanted to get into a big to-do with her family, but she didn't see a way out of this one. "Okay. You can drop me off at the sheriff's office. I want to talk to Seth anyway."

Both her mom and dad looked relieved.

"He'll be glad. He's so worried that you're angry with him," Holly said.

Callie managed another small smile. "Why would I be angry with him for loving me?"

Holly enfolded Callie in her arms and hugged her tight. "You'll come back tonight and stay? Your dads are cooking your favorite."

Again the lie escaped so easily. "Of course. I'll drive up after I get my truck."

Ethan grabbed the keys and put an arm around Callie to guide her out the door. She climbed into the Land Rover and stared over the land, her parents' home, all the things she loved most. She avoided the meadow. She couldn't even look at it now.

Her dad was quiet as they pulled down the driveway toward the mountain road. She focused her attention straight ahead, refusing to glimpse at the land that had meant so much to her.

"I wish I knew what to say," her dad said. "I hate to see you hurting so much, baby girl."

She turned to look at him. "Tell me what happened. I need to know. With the meadow, I mean."

He looked discomfited, as if he had no desire to cause her more distress. When she continued to stare at him, he sighed.

"It's true we tried to buy the land for years. The owner's name was Jacob Hancock. It's also true it had been Hancock land for much longer than we've been here. We slowly bought up the land around us to expand our holdings, but he always refused to sell. Said it had been part of his family for generations and he was holding onto it for his son and daughter."

Callie swallowed but she held her jaw firm, determined that she'd not show one iota of emotion.

"Your mother loved the meadow. We persisted. Once a year we'd approach Hancock about selling. He never would. We finally gave up about a year before your mother found out she was pregnant with you. We figured we'd never lay our hands on it.

"Then a few months before we found out about you, Hancock's wife came to see Adam. Said her husband had passed away, she had two young children to raise and that she needed the money. She was visibly upset and worried. I got the impression that his passing had been a shock both emotionally...and financially. She hinted that he'd hidden some of his financial difficulty from her and that she thought they were better off than they were in reality. When he died, she discovered that she basically had nothing.

"We talked about it. We wanted the land, and we could afford more than fair price. We paid her twice what it was worth because she had those kids to raise and we wanted her to be provided for. You know the rest."

Callie nodded. Yes, she did. They'd surprised her mom with the land when she was pregnant with Callie and then Callie had been born there.

All this time Max had hated and resented her family for taking what he considered his. He believed her dads had leaned on his mom after his stepfather had died.

It appalled her.

Her dads were the most honorable men she knew.

How could someone be so cold and calculating as to track her down in Europe and execute a planned seduction? It was more than simple seduction. He'd lied to her. He'd demanded her submission. Was it all an elaborate charade? Was he even someone who craved dominance and submission or had he simply seen it as a way to get what he wanted?

The worst lie of all. He'd told her he loved her and talked about their children, for God's sake.

She swallowed the rage and grief and curled her fingers into tight fists.

"I'm so sorry, baby girl. So sorry that you had to be involved in his fight against us. It kills me that someone used you because of a misunderstanding with me and your dads."

She shook her head adamantly. "It's not your fault, Dad. It's mine. I let him use me. I let him manipulate me. That's on me. Never you."

Ethan looked like he'd argue further, but she simply turned her head and stared out the window as they drew closer to town.

When they pulled up at the sheriff's department, she breathed a sigh of relief when she didn't see Seth's truck out front. He was out on a call.

She turned to her dad and then leaned across the seat to hug him. "Thank you. I'll just wait here for Seth to come back, and then I'll get my truck and go out to Lily's for a while."

"I can stay with you."

"No. You go. I'm okay."

He reluctantly nodded.

She started to get out but then she stopped and turned back. "I love you, Dad. And thanks. For everything."

He smiled. "Love you too, baby girl. I'll see you later."

She nodded and then closed the door. She waited until her dad drove back down the street before she started toward the bank. It took a little longer than she would have liked. Apparently cleaning out a savings account and converting to traveler's checks wasn't an everyday occurrence. Or at least not in Clyde.

Half an hour later, she walked out and tensed when she saw Seth's truck parked on the street in front of the sheriff's department. By now she was certain he'd know she was coming. Her mom and dads had likely been on the phone to let him know.

And she still had to see the realtor.

Hoping Seth would be patient and not come looking for her, she ducked into Clyde's only real estate office.

An hour later and after much arguing with Janice, Callie walked out of the office with an envelope tucked under her arm. She headed down the sidewalk to the sheriff's office and stepped inside where she was greeted by the receptionist who waved her on to Seth's office.

She hesitated outside the door but then knocked softly.

"It's open," Seth called.

She pushed in and Seth shot to his feet when he saw her

standing in the doorway.

"Hi," she said quietly.

He hurried around and without a word, enfolded her in a bone-crushing hug. "I've been so worried."

She smiled as she pulled away. "I just came by because I wanted you to know I'm not angry with you."

He stood back, his gaze taking in her bedraggled appearance. "You look like shit."

Trust her big brother to be blunt.

"I feel like shit," she said honestly. "But I'll get over it."

He put his hand out to touch her cheek. "I'm sorry, Callie. For a lot of things."

She shook her head. "Don't be. I just wanted you to know I love you, and I know you did what you thought was best. You were trying to protect me. I don't hate you for that."

"I'm glad. I handled it badly. I was pissed. I'd just gotten my report an hour before we left to go up for lunch. I saw red. Now I wish I'd done things differently."

"The outcome would still be the same," she said softly.

"Want me to kill him?"

She shook her head sadly. "No. I want you to forget he exists. It's what I plan to do."

She started to back toward the door. "Tell Lily I love her, will you?"

Seth's brows drew together. "You can tell her yourself. Aren't you going out to see her?"

"Tell her anyway."

She walked back through the door before Seth could do or say anything else. When she got outside, she put the envelope between her teeth and dug into her purse for the tiny silver key that Max had given her when he placed the bands around her wrists.

There was still one more person she had to see before she left town.

Chapter Twenty-Seven

The knock at Max's hotel room door startled him from his dark thoughts. He bolted to his feet, his pulse racing a mile a minute as he rushed to open it.

He flung the door open to see Callie standing there staring at him with dull, dead eyes.

Her appearance shocked him. She was still wearing the same clothes as she had when they'd driven to her parents' together. Her hair was limp, half covering her face. She looked exhausted. Her eyes were rimmed with red, her lips were drawn into a pale, thin line.

She looked liked death. She looked exactly like he felt.

"Callie," he whispered past cracked lips.

Oh God, he wanted to pull her into his arms. He wanted to hold her and kiss her and tell her he'd never let anything bad ever touch her again. He wanted to say he was sorry, but the words—the damn words—were hopelessly inadequate. How could he possibly put into words what was bleeding from his heart?

She held out a large manila envelope that bulged at the bottom. Her fingers shook, making the envelope flap like a breeze blew it.

"This is for you," she said in a low voice.

"Callie, come in. Please."

He would have reached for her but she shrank back as if anticipating such a move. She looked so infinitely fragile that he was afraid to demand—or ask—anything at all.

So he curled his fingers into tight fists at his sides as he tempered the urge to haul her into his arms and never let go.

She shook her head. "I can't stay. I have to go. But I wanted—" Her voice cracked and she swallowed visibly.

She shoved the envelope toward him again, hitting him in the chest with it until he had no choice but to take it from her.

"It's yours. I can't..." Tears filled her eyes, and she lost the tightly held control that had made her face an unbreakable shield.

Her features crumpled and tears slid endlessly down her cheeks.

"I can't... It's ruined for me. I can't even bear to look at it. You've ruined that for me. It's not mine. It can never be mine because I can't even be there without thinking of you. Of what you did. It's not my safe place anymore. It will always represent hell and what I lost—what was never mine."

She took a step back and he panicked. His chest was so tight he felt like he'd explode. There was such grief. Such finality to her words and her actions.

This was her goodbye. He couldn't let her go. Never.

"Callie, please, you have to listen to me."

She shook her head in denial and turned and fled toward the parking lot. He flung the envelope aside and rushed after her, his pulse exploding at his temples.

She fled like a spooked deer. Her truck door was open, the engine was running, as if she'd anticipated just such a flight. She was inside and backing out of the parking spot before her door even closed.

He hit the side of her door with his body, his hands pressed against her window as he shouted her name over and over.

She paused only to put it in gear and she looked at him. Just once, her face so tormented, hurt so bright in her eyes that he wanted to die on the spot.

"Callie, *please*. Don't do this!"

She looked forward and accelerated, leaving him standing in the parking lot, shouting her name.

He stared after her, so numb, so frozen that he couldn't process what had just occurred. He couldn't let her go. Not this way.

He slapped at his pants pockets and cursed, realizing his keys were in his room. He sprinted back, determined to go after her. Make her listen. Beg her for forgiveness. Again.

When he ran through the still-open doorway, the envelope that she'd pushed into his chest lay on the floor. He stopped and stared, a sick feeling rising in his gut. What had she meant?

What had she *done*?

He slowly bent down to retrieve the envelope and walked over to the bed where his keys rested on the nightstand. With shaking hands, he tore open the seal and reached inside for the sheaf of papers.

It took him three attempts before he could make sense of the wording. At the bottom, her signature, barely a scrawl, made it official.

"Oh God," he whispered. "Callie, no. No."

She'd given him Callie's Meadow. All it lacked was his signature to make it legal.

On the bed, the envelope lay, the bulge still at the bottom.

His heart aching, he clumsily shook out the contents and there on the sheets, gleaming in the soft light were the two bands he'd placed around her wrists.

He closed his eyes. They burned like fire. Raw and scratchy like the insides of his lids were lined with sandpaper. Tears gathered. Tears that he hadn't shed when his stepfather had died. Or when his mother had passed away so unexpectedly.

He'd been strong then. First for his mother and sister. A rock for them to lean on. He'd held them while they cried. And then when his mother had passed he'd been there for his sister.

There was no one here for him now. Callie was gone. She hated him. He'd destroyed something infinitely fragile and so very precious.

He looked down at the paper in his hand. The words blurred and then a tear fell onto her scrawled signature.

The land was his. His promise fulfilled. And he'd never felt so damn empty in his life.

Chapter Twenty-Eight

Max hadn't slept in two nights. He was surly. He was pissed. He missed Callie so damn much that he ached.

He'd resorted to prowling around town looking for her, acting like a damn stalker again. But he hadn't seen her, hadn't seen her truck. Hadn't even seen a single damn family member of hers.

Enough was enough. He was going to go up that mountain, and he didn't give a shit if he had to take on the entire Colter clan, he wasn't leaving until he talked some sense into her.

He showered, shaved and dressed just so he wouldn't look like some escapee from prison, and then he walked out to get into his car. Right now he didn't care if he got his ass kicked so hard he wound up in the hospital, just as long as he was able to pin Callie down in one place long enough to wipe that horrible look of pain and betrayal from her eyes.

God, he never wanted to see such a look on her face for the rest of his life. If she'd let him, if she'd just give him a chance, he'd make damn sure nothing—especially him—ever hurt her again.

Just as he was getting into his car, he glanced up and saw Lily Colter walk out of the sheriff's department and down the sidewalk toward the small grocery store.

His pulse ratcheted up. He slammed his door and sprinted

across the street to intercept Callie's sister-in-law.

When she looked up and saw him, she took an instinctive step back. Her eyes hardened and her lips curled into a snarl. For such a small, dainty woman, she could look damn mean.

He put out a placating hand. "Lily, please. I need your help."

Her glare froze him to the nuts.

"Look, I know you think I'm the biggest asshole on earth, but I have to talk to Callie. Is she up at her parents'?"

The anger in Lily's eyes faded and the same raw grief he'd witnessed in Callie's eyes now stared back at him.

"She's gone."

His brows furrowed. "Gone? What do you mean gone?"

Lily stepped forward, her fist balled like she'd love nothing more than to hit him. "She left. Cleaned out her bank account, all the money she'd saved for her dream house. She's off somewhere and we don't know where. She's out there hurting. Devastated. And we can't help her because she's gone. Because of *you*. Because of what you did to her."

His stomach fell. His chest caved in as a wave of despair nearly crippled him. He had to grip the light post to keep his knees from buckling.

"No," he said hoarsely. "Oh God, no. I have to find her."

Tears shimmered in Lily's gaze. "Good luck with that. All we know is that she flew out of Denver on a nonstop flight to London. She could be anywhere right now. Callie doesn't stay in hotels. She doesn't travel like most people. She'll disappear for weeks—months at a time. Then one day she'll come home. I hope and pray she comes home this time. Her entire family is devastated."

He stared at the woman and didn't even try to hide the

horrible grief festering inside him. “Lily, I love her. I *love* her. Do you understand that? Things happened so fast. I never had the chance to explain. But God, I love her so damn much.”

Lily gazed at him for a long moment until finally her expression softened. “Then why? If you love her so much, why?”

“I was never going to go after her meadow. I couldn’t. Not once I met her—fell in love with her—saw how much that land meant to her. But that is why I searched her out. I’m damned by my own actions, but things changed after I met her. I swear to you they did.”

Lily put her hand on Max’s arm. Her touch was so gentle that he wanted her hand to stay there. It was the only soft thing in his world right now. His only comfort where he had none.

“Then you have to find her, Max. And you have to tell her. You have to make her listen. It won’t be easy. I’m not sure she’ll listen this time.”

Max took Lily’s hand and raised it to his lips to press a brief kiss across her knuckles. “Thank you, Lily. For listening. It means more than you’ll ever know.”

She smiled ruefully. “My husbands will tell you my heart is too soft for my own good. Callie will tell you I have a vicious streak that she loves. I’ll fully admit, what I really wanted to do was kick you in the balls. But I can’t fault you for loving her. And I believe you when you say you do.”

Max smiled for the first time since everything had gone to hell. “I think you’re a very special lady, Lily.”

“Just find her and bring her home to us,” Lily said softly.

For the first three weeks after Callie’s departure, Max spared no expense in his efforts to locate her. The problem was, as Lily had said, Callie wasn't most people. She didn't check into hotels. She didn't often stay in one place for more than a day. He only had London as a starting point, and all he'd been able to determine was that she took the Star to Paris. After she reached the continent, she could literally be anywhere.

He didn't eat. Didn't sleep. He was consumed with finding Callie so he could bring her home. Or not bring her home. He didn't care as long as he could find her and confront her.

It was nearly a month before he realized that his efforts were misdirected. Callie wouldn't be found if she didn't want to be. But eventually she'd come home, wouldn't she? He didn't believe for a minute that she wouldn't return to the family she loved more than anything.

It was then he realized that he needed to focus his efforts on making her homecoming special.

And that precipitated a trip up the mountain to see her family.

With a little help on the sly from Lily, he made damn sure that the entire family would be assembled when he arrived. It was time to take the bull by the horns. It wouldn't be pretty, but he wasn't about to give up without one hell of a fight.

He parked by the myriad of vehicles and got out, spoiling for a fight. He strode to the front door and knocked briskly.

He didn't have to wait long. The door opened and Adam Colter stood there unsmiling, his steady gaze brewing with anger.

"What the hell are you doing here?"

Knowing he wouldn't get through the door without a little shock value, Max thrust the document that Callie had signed at her father.

"We need to talk about this."

Adam took the paper and scanned the contents. His expression grew darker and darker until he resembled a black cloud of fury.

"You son of a bitch," Adam seethed. "I'll fight you on this. It will never hold up in court. She signed this under duress and great emotional strain. When I'm through with you, the entire world will know what a calculating bastard you are."

Max held up his hand. "I don't give a shit what that paper says or whether it will hold up in court. I never intend to sign it or pursue ownership."

Adam paused and then looked back up at Max, open speculation in his gaze.

"Like I said, we need to talk. Preferably without violence, although after three weeks of searching all over Europe for your daughter, I'm about ready to shed some blood. Yours will do just fine."

Adam continued to stare at him for a long moment, and a glimmer of a smile shadowed on his lips. "You love my daughter."

"Yeah, what was your first clue?"

"You can cut the sarcasm, son. Your actions haven't been those of a man who loves a woman."

"Just let me in so we can talk about this. I want things to be perfect if and when Callie comes home."

Adam hesitated a moment. "I didn't take advantage of your mother, Max. I can show you the letter she sent me. I can show you the bill of sale. I paid her more than a fair price. The last thing my brothers and I wanted was to take advantage of a young widow with two children to raise."

Max swallowed and then slowly nodded his acceptance. He had to let go of his anger. These were Callie's dads. The past couldn't be changed. He'd been a boy when his mother had sold, and he'd viewed the transaction through the eyes of an angry child. It was time to consider that he'd been wrong. He'd been wrong about so many other things.

"I owe you and your brothers an apology," Max said in a low voice.

"If you make my daughter happy again, that's all the apology we need."

"Thank you, sir. I plan to do exactly that."

Adam stepped back and then motioned Max inside. Max walked past him and into the living room where all of Callie's family was assembled.

Lily met his gaze and shot him a look of sympathy about the time the rest of the room exploded into chaos.

It took a full five minutes for Adam to calm everyone down. Even Holly stood to the side, her face drawn into tight lines of anger—and grief.

He went to her first, wanting to ease her fears, her worries, even when he didn't have any information to do so.

"Have you found her?" Lily asked just as he approached Holly Colter.

Max turned to look at Lily's hopeful face, his own drawn into an unhappy grimace. "No, I haven't."

Then he turned back to Callie's mother. "I want to apologize to you for all the hurt I've caused. I love your daughter. I love her more than I've ever loved anyone else. I've done nothing for the last three weeks but try to find her. I've come to the realization that she'll come home when she's ready, and when she does, I want things to be...right."

Adam handed the paper to Holly. "He brought this."

Holly scanned the paper and then her eyes filled with tears.

"No. Tell me this isn't real."

Max took the paper from her shaking hand and then calmly ripped it into a dozen tiny pieces. "I don't care if it was real or not. It doesn't matter because I won't sign it."

"Thank God," Holly whispered.

"Someone want to tell us what the hell is going on?" Seth demanded from across the room.

Max turned to face the forbidding faces of the Colter men.

"Callie tried to give me her meadow. I won't accept it. I love her. I'm not going to lose her without a fight. You need to accept that. She loves you. You love her. I love her. There has to be room for all of us in her life if she chooses it. I'm here to make my peace with you, but I'm also here because I need your help."

Silence fell and perplexed looks replaced the anger of just moments before.

"What do you have in mind?" Ryan Colter asked cautiously.

"All Callie's ever wanted is to build her dream house. She takes ridiculously low-paying, dangerous jobs and she saves. She drives a truck that's about to fall apart, and she doesn't even have a home of her own because she saves every penny for that dream.

"She took that money she's been saving and she left. She gave up on that dream. I'm going to give it back to her."

"Okay," Ethan said slowly. "How do you propose to do that?"

"I'm going to build her house in that meadow so that she has it to come home to. Whether she takes me back or not, I want her to have that safe place—a place of her own. Something she can always come back to no matter where she travels or where her path takes her. But I can't do it without your help."

Again, heavy silence descended, as they seemed to grapple

with what he'd said. Grudging admiration and maybe even respect entered their eyes.

Her brothers eased back into their seats. Lily smiled over at Max. He smiled back and mouthed a silent *thank you.*

Callie's dads also settled on the couches, and Holly walked over to sit between Adam and Ethan.

"What can we do to help?" Adam asked.

"I need you to help me build her dream. She's spoken to me some about it so I have an idea of what she wants. But I need anything you have. Any tidbit of what she's talked about. What she likes. How she'd want it built."

"I drew her a picture," Lily spoke up. "I drew the outside to her specifications. I still have a copy. I can give you that."

"That would be fantastic, Lily. Thank you."

"You're serious about this?" Seth asked. There was a glimmer of doubt, a look of incredulity etched on his brow. "You're going to give up the meadow without a fight?"

"The meadow is Callie's," Max said in an even voice. "I'll never fight her for it. What I won't give up without a fight is...Callie."

"I'm handy with tools," Dillon said, speaking for the first time. "I built my own place. I'll do what I can."

"I appreciate it. I'm going to have a team of contractors up here. No expense will be spared. I can use any input or information you all have."

"You really do love her," Holly said in a soft voice.

Max looked from one family member to the next until finally his gaze rested on Callie's mother. "She's my life."

"Well, let's get cracking," Ryan said. "We've got a house to build."

Chapter Twenty-Nine

Callie put her truck into gear and began the drive up the mountain. Autumn had come to the mountains and everywhere around her, aspens burst with gold so vibrant that it hurt her eyes to look at the shimmering leaves.

Already there was a chill to the air that bespoke winter's impending arrival. She turned up the heat and prayed it still worked.

The long months away had taken their toll. In some ways, it seemed she'd been gone a lifetime, but in other ways, it was just yesterday.

She missed her family and she longed to be in the middle of them again.

And Max.

How she'd wanted the passage of time to dim the hurt, but her heart was as torn as it had been the day she left.

She forced her gaze forward as she approached her meadow. No, it wasn't hers any longer. It was Max's. She hoped it gave him peace. It had given her none.

Her lips trembled as she passed the turnoff that would wind its way to the valley below. Out of the corner of her eye, she saw something that made her brake in the middle of the road.

She whipped her head around, her mouth falling open. He couldn't. He wouldn't.

Pain shredded her throat and stabbed deep into her soul. He'd built a house in the meadow. He hadn't wasted any time taking it over and making it his.

Tears burned her eyelids and she closed her eyes, determined to look away.

It was like a train wreck. She was compelled to open her eyes and stare down at the cabin nestled on the banks of the creek.

God, it was *her* house. *Her* dream house.

Was there no end to the ways he could make her bleed?

She jammed the gearshift into reverse and accelerated until she got back to the turnoff for the meadow. She roared down the road until she reached the place where she and Max had stopped that night so many months ago. A lifetime ago.

She got out and slowly walked a few feet in front of her truck.

The old wooden fence was gone. Maybe he planned to put up a new one. A separation of Wilder land from Colter land.

She was a fool. How could she ever come back here when she'd be faced with Max at every turn? How could her parents' house, always a haven—*home*—be a refuge when she would be forced to face so much pain and betrayal simply by looking out her window?

No, she couldn't come back here.

"Callie."

She froze as Max's soft voice slid over her ears like a warm, comforting blanket. She closed her eyes and squeezed her fingers into tight balls. Not this. Anything but this. Hadn't she bled enough?

She hadn't heard his approach. But then she'd been too ensconced in the agony of seeing her dream belong to someone else.

"Callie, please. Look at me."

The soft entreaty was nearly her undoing. Despite the fact that the last thing she wanted was to confront Max again, she found herself slowly turning, responding to the command layered into his quiet request.

He looked different. Haggard. He'd lost weight. There were lines of fatigue etched into his brow and dark shadows rimmed his eyes. He looked...terrible.

"Thank God you're home."

"How did you know?" she demanded. "How could you possibly have found me this fast? I only just got into town."

His lip curled, and a blaze of anger flashed in his eyes.

"Because I've waited every goddamn day for the last three months for you to come back. I've had the entire goddamn town on alert. Everyone has been watching for you—waiting. I got a phone call as soon as your truck was spotted in Clyde. I came as soon as I got the call. I was only a quarter mile behind you."

"Why?" she asked helplessly.

"Because you're mine, Callie, and I'm not letting you go."

She whirled around so that her back was to him and she stared out over the meadow again. "It's beautiful," she managed to grind out.

"I want you to see it," he said, closer this time as he walked up behind her.

She shook her head. Even Max couldn't be this cruel.

"Yes, Callie. You're going to come with me and you're going to see the house."

He took her hand and pulled her toward the path leading

down the hillside. His fingers were like iron digits around hers. No escape. No choice but to follow him.

She walked stiffly, each step making her want to cry out for him to stop.

"Why are you doing this?"

Max paused only for a moment as he turned back to stare at her. "This is yours, Callie. It's all for you. Every last piece of wood. Every nail. Every coat of paint. Every flower planted in the boxes out front. It's all yours. Your dream. Just the way you wanted it."

Her mouth fell open and she stumbled after him as he continued dragging her closer to the house.

As they neared, she took in the large log cabin. Tears swam in her eyes, making the house go blurry. God, it was exactly what she'd designed in her head. How could he know? She'd told him a little about her house. Odds and ends. But how could he possibly have built something that was straight out of her heart?

They stood in front of the stone steps leading to the front door. He gestured toward the exterior. "This was taken straight from the picture that Lily drew for you. Every inch down to the planters and the species of flowers. Even the cedar porch swing and the welcome sign. Read it, Callie. Tell me what it says."

Her gaze drifted to the words on the worn piece of wood—just as she'd imagined it—standing on an old post just beside the steps to the front porch.

"Welcome to Callie's Meadow," she whispered.

"That's right, Callie. Your meadow."

She glanced up at Max, so flabbergasted, so utterly undone, she couldn't even form the words. "I don't understand."

"Come inside," he said.

He pulled at her hand and they trudged up the steps. He unlocked the door and swung it open into a large living room with a giant stone fireplace that took up the back wall.

Everywhere she looked, she saw her dreams come to life. All the daydreams. Every detail was carefully rendered. It was her dream house.

"It's yours, Callie. The whole thing. The land. The house. It all belongs to you."

She swallowed the growing knot in her throat only to choke and cough as emotion swelled and took a stranglehold. How could she be happy with her dream when it wasn't complete? How could she be happy here without the man she'd imagined at her side, in her bed, holding her in front of that gigantic fireplace on cold nights?

Tears slipped down her cheeks. Tears she hadn't shed in months. Tears she didn't think she had to shed anymore.

"Why, Max? Why did you do this?"

He turned to face her, his eyes so tormented that she caught her breath.

"Because I love you, Callie. I love you so damn much I can't even breathe. I can't eat. I can't sleep. All I can do is work on this house and hope like hell that you'll come home and see how much I love you and give me another chance."

He took her hands and held them so tight her fingers went numb. But she didn't pull them away. She stared, so afraid to hope, so afraid to believe that her head hurt.

"I never got to tell you everything, Callie. I never got to explain. I told the truth—a truth that forever damned me in your eyes. But I didn't get to tell you the rest."

"What's the rest?" she whispered.

"It's true that I tracked you down in Europe. Hell, I don't even know what my plan was. I was frustrated because I was getting nowhere with your fathers, and so I was going to go straight to the source. Meet you, let you put a face to the name, tell you my story and hope to hell you'd agree to sell. It was absolutely my intention to do whatever it took to get you to agree."

She closed her eyes and tried to look away, but Max's hands tightened around hers and he pulled so she'd look back at him.

"But then I met you, Callie. I met you and fell so hard for you that I never knew what hit me. I only knew I wanted to make you mine. I forgot all about the meadow. About my promise to my stepfather that I'd keep it in our family and hand it down to my children so they could hand it down to theirs. I forgot all about my honor or what I felt like my obligation was to my family."

He paused and then took a deep breath before continuing.

"Then I got that call from my sister that my mom was dying. I was so conflicted. How could I have allowed myself to become so distracted, so utterly involved with you that I'd ignored everything else in my life? I pulled back. I pulled way back. I didn't call you. I didn't return. My mom died and her last words were an apology to me and my sister for selling our legacy. She begged me to get it back, and I felt so guilty because I made her a promise I never had any intention of keeping.

"And then I knew I had to find you again. For me there was no other option. I was going to do whatever I had to in order to get you back, and I'll be honest, I never wanted you to know the real reason we'd met. I would have never told you because I never wanted to hurt you so badly."

He lifted her hands and looked deep into her eyes, his own

blazing with sincerity.

"I never intended to coerce you or even ask you to sell the land. I had to make a choice between having you or keeping a promise I'd made to my family. I chose you, Callie. I chose *you.*"

She stared back at him, her mind in such turmoil that she didn't even know what to say. How to respond. How could she tell him that she *wanted* to believe him? Oh God, she wanted to believe him with everything she had. But how could she? How could she risk everything...again?

Max watched the obvious conflict cross her face. How could he be blind to it? He sucked in his breath and then he lowered her hands, gently letting them go.

Then he backed away, just a few steps, enough that there was space between them. And then he slowly sank to his knees on the polished wood floor.

She stared in shock—in absolute horror—as he went to his knees in front of her, his hands turned up, resting on the tops of his thighs. He bowed his head in front of her and simply waited.

Then he spoke. His voice trembled. There was such emotion clogging his throat that she could barely hear him.

"I'm begging you, Callie. Give me another chance. I'll never ask for more than you're willing to give. I'll take whatever you're capable of giving me."

"Oh Max. No. Oh no, no, no," she whispered.

She fell to her knees in front of him, pushing at him with her hands, trying to force him back to his feet. Max was never a man to kneel, to submit, to *beg.* Not this man. Not her Max.

Tears streamed down her cheeks and sobs tore from her throat, the sound so anguished that it made her wince.

"Don't do this, Max. Stand up. Please. Not on your knees. I

don't want this. Don't do this to yourself. To us."

He lifted his haunted gaze to meet hers. Then he reached for her shoulders and pulled her to him.

"Don't you understand, Callie? I belong to you. Only you. You gave yourself to me before, but now I'm giving you myself. I just want you to say you can love me again. Maybe not today. Or even tomorrow. But one day. Until then, I'll love you enough for both of us."

She threw her arms around him, nearly knocking him to the floor. She sobbed noisily against his neck. She probably got snot and God knows what else all over his shirt. She didn't care.

"I love you today, Max. *Today.* And tomorrow. And the next day. A year from now. A decade from now. When we're both old and gray and toothless, I'll still love you."

He crushed her to him. His arms held her so tightly that she couldn't move—she didn't want to. His entire body shook, and he just held on to her as she cried.

"Thank God," he whispered. "Thank God. I love you so damn much, Callie. I'm nothing without you. Please tell me that we'll live together in your dream house. It was yours before but somehow in the building of this, of making all your daydreams a reality, it became my dream too. I want to live it with you."

She squeezed him for a long moment because she couldn't speak around the sobs knotting her throat. He rubbed his hands up and down her back and rocked her back and forth.

"I just want to be with you," she whispered. "That's my dream, Max. Not this house. Not this land. Just you."

He pulled her away and smoothed the ragged strands of hair from her face. "And you're my dream, Callie. Always. You loving me. Me loving you. That's enough. It's all I want. It's all I'll ever want."

She smiled. God, it felt so good to smile and know that the world was finally right. Then she leaned forward and kissed him.

Their lips melted together like snow in the middle of a thaw. He kissed her hungrily. Breathlessly. With so much love and emotion that her chest ached with it.

Then she merely rested her forehead against his as they struggled to catch their breath. He touched her. She touched him. Two lovers reunited after a long separation.

"Your family is worried. We need to go see them," he said.

She pulled away, startled by his statement.

He grinned. "I think you'll find that your family and I have come to an...understanding. They love you. I love you. It's common ground no one can argue."

She closed her eyes, dangerously close to tears all over again. Euphoria settled over her. After so long of being weighted down by grief and sadness, the jolt of happiness that surged through her veins was intoxicating.

She wanted to yell. She wanted to jump up and down. She wanted to tell the entire world that life was...perfect.

"What do you say we trek over to your folks' place and let them hug you and welcome you home, and then we can come back here and try out the new bed in the master bedroom."

She slipped her hand into his and let him pull her to her feet. She smiled up at him, her heart near to bursting.

"I'd like that. I'd like that a lot."

"And just so you know, Lily and your mother have been planning our wedding for two months now. I think they all saw just how determined I was never to let you go."

She laughed. "I'm okay with that. I'm very okay with that."

As Max pulled her toward the door, he turned back to her and smiled. The shadows in his eyes lifted and were replaced by so much joy that it took her breath away.

"So how's next week sound to you?"

About the Author

Maya Banks lives in Texas with her husband, three children and assortment of cats. When she's not writing, she can be found hunting, fishing or playing poker. A southern girl born and bred, Maya loves life below the Mason Dixon, and more importantly, loves bringing southern characters and settings to life in her stories.

Check Maya's website out at: www.mayabanks.com

Email Maya: maya@mayabanks.com

Find Maya on Facebook: facebook.com/AuthorMayaBanks

Or follow Maya on Twitter: twitter.com/maya_banks